KATHRYN SPRANDIO ELLS

Please Read Me

First published by Kindle Direct Publishing 2023

Copyright © 2023 by Kathryn Sprandio Ells

All rights reserved. No part of this publication may be reproduced, stored or transmitted in any form or by any means, electronic, mechanical, photocopying, recording, scanning, or otherwise without written permission from the publisher. It is illegal to copy this book, post it to a website, or distribute it by any other means without permission.

First edition

This book was professionally typeset on Reedsy.
Find out more at reedsy.com

To my Mom, who once said, "You're good at writing. Why don't you try that?"
To Zach, what the hell are you doing in the bathroom day and night?
To my babies, my greatest creative creations.
MSJA, CHC, AU: thanks for teaching me words & giving me the courage to share them.

Contents

Preface		ii
Acknowledgement		iii
1	This is a Poem	1
2	The Club	2
3	Love Under the Monkey Bars	15
4	First Lust	22
5	First Kiss	24
6	She'll Pay	32
7	The Cut	34
8	Pending	38
9	Mocha Frapp with Tears	49
10	His Roommate Walter	54
11	A Text Message	56
12	One More	64
13	Traffic	71
14	Brush Burn	81
15	Digital Love	101
About the Author		102

Preface

Hi, I'm Kathryn. Thanks for stopping by.

The stories within these pages were written for my creative writing program. After putting them aside for ten years, I decided it was time to share them with the world. My hope is that people other than just my Mom have bought this book. Hi, Mom. Thanks for reading.

Each piece is a work of fiction, but the narrators all have a little bit of my personality sewn into theirs. Life isn't easy, but we all do it and it's awkward for everyone. Relationships are messy and feelings are complex. The neuroses of the characters are relatable and charming. At least, I think they are. It's not at all annoying. It's totally funny, but heartfelt. But, listen to me, blabbering on. I'll let you find out for yourself.

Without further ado, Please Read Me and please, enjoy!

Acknowledgement

I must acknowledge my Aunt Clare and my dear friend Andréa Fernandes for running through this with a fine tooth comb. You gals certainly know how to make a collection of stories feel good about themselves. What is a piece of writing without its editors? Bad writing!

1

This is a Poem

This is a poem
About a guy I once dated.
I liked him.
But then I didn't like him.
I dumped him.
He threw up.
A squirrel ate it.
This is the end of the poem.

2

The Club

It was a rainy Tuesday in November. The clouds above blanketed the sky with a rich dark gray color. The smell of the air was ominous. Mother Nature was warning me of things to come.

"The big 'change' may occur this year for some of you girls," Mrs. Brindle said.

The big "change." I squirmed in my seat when she said the word "change." Change is frightening. I had a nervous breakdown when my favorite after school show changed from its 3 o'clock spot to 4 o'clock. It wasn't the same an hour later and most importantly my after school routine was ruined. I would get home at 2:55, get a handful of Oreos, a glass of milk, and watch my show. I couldn't eat Oreos at 4 o'clock, that was way too close to dinnertime.

"This is an exciting time for all of you," Mrs. Brindle said with a large Penny Wise smile across her face.

"You're going to become women soon. You'll notice changes in yourself over the next couple years, some will be external and others will be internal. You'll feel uncomfortable, but it's important to remember, everything you are going through is natural."

As she explained, she put a video in the VCR of the TV in the front of the room.

On a normal day, when the TV was brought out the class would erupt in excitement. Getting a video break from a lecture was like being given water after wandering the desert. This time, however, the atmosphere was bleak. The boys were sent down to play in the gym, so it was the eight of us girls awaiting a twenty-five minute video that would reveal our fate.

My Mom had mentioned a little bit about the big "change" when I was younger, but she never went into full detail. I'm the only girl in my family. I have four brothers, so the topic of female organs wasn't a common one. I had overheard my Mom talking about it with her sisters once when she was complaining about cramps. I also remember when I was in third grade I heard my Mom say to my Dad that she needed more pads.

* * *

"Hon, I'm going to the market, need anything?" My Dad asked as he walked to the front door. I was in the living room doing my math homework.

"Yeah, grab some pads please," my Mom responded in a whisper.

I noticed my Dad's eyes roll as he went out of the door. I was puzzled by my Mom's request.

"Mom, I have plenty of pads of paper upstairs if you need them."

"What?"

"You told Dad you need pads. I have some upstairs."

She laughed as she walked into the living room and knelt down beside me.

"I didn't mean pads of paper. They're big girl pads. You'll understand when you're older."

Then a few days later, I caught her crying in the living room while watching TV. It wasn't a sad show or anything; it was a Kleenex commercial.

"Mom? What's wrong?" I started to tear up because whenever I see her cry, I want to cry.

"Nothing sweetie. Mommies cry sometimes for no reason."

I sat down and cuddled up on the sofa with her and we cried together.

* * *

"Does anyone know what this 'change' is called?" Mrs. Brindle looked around, all of us silent. Her eyes stopped on me.

"Annie, do you know the correct name for this?"

My cheeks blushed. My eyes darted around the room. The other girls had their heads down.

"Um, yeah. I've heard the word before. Is it our minstrel cycle?"

She smiled. "Close enough, it's menstrual. A minstrel is a medieval poet or musician."

My friends giggled.

"Oh, right, menstrual." I threw my head down and stared at my thumbs.

"Yes, girls, it's your menstrual cycle. Today we're going to watch a video that will explain everything in full detail."

The world seemed to go in slow motion when she said "full detail."

"If we don't have time for questions at the end, you can see me whenever you feel the need. Also, the nurse is always available."

I watched her finger make its way to the play button, sweat beaded up on my forehead.

"Menstruation and Me: What it Means to be a Woman," said the narrator. Little female organs bounced around the screen as the title came into focus accompanied by elevator music.

"A common term for menstruation is called a 'period,' like the punctuation mark."

The narrator, a young woman wearing a gray pantsuit with a jacket with large shoulder pads, smiled and put her hand up; a large black period popped up on the screen. I stared long and hard at that period, the period that marks the end of my childhood. Why did they call it a period? A period indicates the end of a thought. This was only the beginning of a lifetime of confusion and pain.

The video consisted of poorly made diagrams of our insides and testimonials from women. I could have made a better video with my Dad's camcorder.

A young girl with a Southern accent stood to the right of the narrator.

"One time, I had my period and my Mom didn't fold my shirt the way I liked it. I started screaming and I threw a lamp against the wall. She said, 'Somebody must have their period.' We all understand each other. It'll be okay."

The narrator put her arm around the girl and nodded. Her grin reminded me of the Joker from Batman.

She threw a lamp against the wall? Is that going to happen to me? If I did that, I don't even want to know what my Mom would do.

Another girl appeared to the left of the narrator. She had an accent that I had never heard.

"I got my first period in the summer. My friends all wanted to go swimming, but I was too shy to tell them what was happening to me. So I simply said I didn't feel well and they didn't question me."

God, I hope I don't get it in the summer. My friends can always tell when I'm lying. What if I get it while swimming in the ocean? Would I attract sharks?

The narrator then told her own tale.

"The first time I got my period I was at a dinner party with my mother. She had to escort me to the bathroom and ask the host for supplies. I exited the bathroom and she announced it to her friends that her baby girl was now a woman. It was a little embarrassing at the time, but I was proud to be entering womanhood."

A little embarrassing? My God, that sounded mortifying. Oh no, I hope my Mom doesn't announce it to everyone. She called everyone she knew when I lost my first tooth. I would need to relocate if my brothers and Dad knew I was becoming a woman.

After the testimonials, a title appeared on the screen, "Periods of the Past." The narrator reappeared next to the title.

"Before sanitary products were created, women would use old clothing, kitchen towels, pretty much any cloth they could find to keep themselves clean. Before adhesive products, women would wear a belt with hooks or clips to keep the cloth in place."

Thank God I don't have to wear a utility belt for five to seven days each month. That's like something a superhero wears. Considering what we're going to be going through, we should be called superheroes. Why don't boys have to endure this kind of pain?

"In some primitive cultures, women were often sent outside to live in a menstrual hut for the duration of their period and bathe in special fountains. In some areas of the world today, these practices are still upheld."

A menstrual hut? I hope I never have to move to wherever they have those. I can't survive in a hut. I can't even handle a night of camping in my backyard.

"We should all consider ourselves very lucky that we are women of the 21st century. We are able to enjoy the accessories that allow us to have happy, healthy periods."

Happy periods? What is happy about any of this? That sounds like an oxymoron. Happy period. Anything involving blood being released on a regular basis shouldn't be considered happy.

After twenty-five minutes of graphic diagrams, over dramatic testimonials, and horrid historical facts, our jaws were hanging like shutters on loose hinges. My basic understanding of this sick process was pieces of me were going to be torn up inside and released for a week once a month. I would feel awful for seven days at the most, four at the least. I would have the urge to cry a lot— I would have horrible cramps, headaches, and bad skin. I would be tired, bloated, and aggressive. I would have an insatiable hunger for chocolate and any other type of junk food, which actually isn't much different from the way I usually am. I could eat junk food forever. I live off of Oreos and cheese curls. Not to mention, I'd be bleeding into a diaper-like device. If you don't want to use a diaper, there was another thing the video described that was shaped like a stick. I can't remember what they called it, something with a T, but I'll call it a lady stick. Anyway, you take your lady stick and just plug it up there.

How is that natural? What if it got lost in there or stuck? Would I have to eat special food? Would I have to have myself strapped down to avoid beating people? I already have meltdowns that cause my whole family to vacate the house. I can't imagine myself throwing a lamp against the wall. And I thought we grew out of diapers. Now we have to wear them again? They're called sanitary napkins, or pads as my Mom calls them, but they're essentially diapers. Diapers that stick to your underwear. That doesn't sound comfortable. And then that stick, that lady stick. That's just wrong. How would I even begin to know how to do that? Would I need a mirror to make sure I was putting it in the right hole? I guess I would feel if it wasn't the right hole. There is nothing sanitary about any of this.

When the movie ended, it was the end of the day. We stood and ran for the door. I was terrified of my body as I walked home. I clutched my stomach imagining a little monster with claws gnawing at my insides.

"Life as you know it will soon end, Annie. Prepare for pain." It laughed like one of those mad scientists on Cartoon Network. I had no way of escaping my fate.

I entered my house and was met by my mother.

"How was school honey?"

"Fine."

I tried to run past her to the safety of my room, but she caught me with one more question.

"What did you learn today?"

I stalled on the stairs and paused before I turned to look at her. What did I learn today? Oh nothing good, just a little tidbit that my body will soon become my own worst enemy causing me hours of excruciating pain once a month and I must endure this until I'm old, but I'm sure you are very familiar with that. By the way, thanks for warning me!

"The usual–Math, English, History. All the stuff you learned."

"Well, that's good." She returned to the kitchen and I fled to my room.

The next day my friends and I met up in the schoolyard at our usual spot.

"I watched a special last night on the menstrual huts on one of my Discovery Channel DVDs," said my friend Jill. "They're real. Men spit at the women and call them monsters, too."

"My older sister told me she knew someone whose period wouldn't stop and she bled to death. The police thought her husband did it. He's in a home now because he went crazy," said Suzy.

"That's not possible. Medically speaking, it knows when to stop. Your body is a well-oiled machine. It knows more about what to do than we do. Plus, Suzy, your sister is crazy. She should be put in a home," Julie said.

"I don't know why all of you want to talk about this," I said. "I doubt it will happen to any of us anytime soon. We're all still young. We have time. And maybe by then there will be new products out that won't be so medieval."

As we conversed about our disgust with nature, Abby, an eighth grader, threw a tennis ball at our circle. It hit me in the back of the head.

"Oh pardon me, Fungus."

* * *

Abby started calling me Fungus when I was in first grade and she was in fourth. I was walking to the nurse's office because I had the chicken pox. I went to school normal and small itchy bumps started popping up during the day. Mrs. Fields noticed me scratching during silent reading time.

"Annie, let me see your arms."

I rolled up the sleeves of my sweater.

"Oh dear," she gasped. "Everyone, back away from Annie. She has something that is very contagious." Mrs. Fields stayed behind her desk. She had never gotten the chicken pox and didn't want to risk it. Apparently, adults can die from chicken pox. I didn't believe it. Death by scratching? Maybe I should have inched closer and we could have gotten a substitute the rest of the year.

"Honey, go ahead and take yourself to the nurse. It's down the hall to the left."

All the kids backed away from me in fear; it didn't help that it was the third day of school. I left the classroom unsure of which way was left. I had had trouble with that since preschool. I stood in the hallway alone scratching at my arms while tears trickled down my cheeks. Each tear burned the little itchy bumps spreading on my arms. I looked all around me to decide which way to go. Abby was leaving the bathroom at the same time. She came up to me with what seemed like an inviting smile on her face.

"Hey, what are you crying for?"

I looked up at this towering figure in front of me. "Something's wrong with me and I don't know where the nurse's office is."

"You poor thing. It's right this way." She took me down the hallway towards the office. "Here it is. What's so wrong that you have to go to the nurse's office?"

She squatted in front of me. I put my arms out. Red splotches were scattered across my arms like connect the dots pictures we were given during free time in the afternoon.

"My goodness, I've seen this before."

"What is it?"

"I'm sorry but you have fungus on your arms."

"Fungus?" I started crying harder.

"Yes, that's right. Dirty people get it. You might lose your arms. If you're lucky, a doctor can cure it before they fall off. Best of luck."

She patted me on the back as she laughed. I cried in the nurse's office, to my Mom's car, all the way to my bedroom. I was convinced for the remainder of the day that my arms would fall off.

* * *

"What are you rejects talking about?"

"Nothing," Betty said. She wasn't afraid to look Abby in the eye like I was.

I picked up her ball and handed it to her and turned my back.

"Exactly, nothing. Because you are nothing."

"Oh good one Abby. Are you such an ignoramus that you can't come up with anything better than that? Is that why you're failing math? You stay up creating useless comebacks instead of doing your homework?" Julie usually stumped Abby with her witty rebuttals.

"Shut it, twerp."

Everybody was a twerp compared to Abby. She was tall with thick arms and legs and a big chest. Even the boys were scared of her. I heard a rumor from some girls in the sixth grade that Abby went through her change abnormally early, the fourth grade. Most people in her class didn't cross over until at least seventh grade. The school nurse used to send girls home with big brown envelopes with a note for their parents. Abby thought she cut her leg at recess and asked her teacher to be excused to the nurse. The nurse told her it was her "change" and gave her the infamous brown envelope and told her to return to class to tell her teacher she had to go home. All the kids in class knew what happened when they saw that brown envelope. The boys teased her the remainder of the year. After that summer, she returned to school three inches taller, her muscles were toned, and her chest was no longer flat. Nobody bothered her after that.

She made our lives hell since we joined the upper schoolyard. There were two schoolyards, an upper and a lower. Grades 1-4 played in the lower, and 5-8 played in the upper. She was the queen.

"I heard you little diseases watched the video yesterday about your big 'change'."

"Yeah, so what's it to you?" Betty stood in front of Abby with her hands on her hips. It was like an image of David and Goliath from the children's Bible Mrs. Brindle kept in the back of the room at the religion table.

"Well, you know if you don't get it by the time you're twelve, it means you're broken. Looks like you little twerps don't have much time. Especially you Fungus, don't you turn twelve in April?"

I turned to face her. "Yeah, but that's not true what you just said. That's stupid. Leave us alone."

"See you later rejects."

She laughed the laugh that made my arms itch. She reminded me of Mrs. Trunchbull from Matilda.

"That's not true guys," Julie said. "I haven't read anything like that in my books. Girls can get it at various ages."

"Julie, give it a rest." I picked up our Frisbee and suggested we play catch.

Once again, I walked home fearing my body. What if Abby was right?

Months passed and my "change" still hadn't occurred. My twelfth birthday was coming up and I had dismissed what Abby told me months ago, but thoughts of it still lingered. I didn't want it to come, but I also didn't want to be broken.

I had gotten into the routine of going to the bathroom more than usual just to be sure it didn't happen. I cut it back when people started to notice.

"Sweetie, are you okay?" my Mom said one night after my fourth trip to the bathroom in a few hours.

"Who? Me? I'm fine. Why?"

"You've been going to the bathroom a lot."

"Oh, that," I said. My eyes darted every which way as I searched my brain for an explanation. "I've been drinking a lot of water lately. Did you know it's recommended that we consume eight glasses a day? I learned it in health class. It's good to stay hydrated. You and Dad should learn from me. You guys drink too much soda. You know you guys could live longer if you drink more water. I want you guys around to see my grandchildren, so drink more water and..."

"Okay," she laughed. "Thanks for the concern."

My friends hadn't crossed over either, so that gave me some relief and after time I didn't check as much.

One morning in March, a week before my birthday, I woke up just like every other day.

"Annie, time to get up."

"Okay," I muttered into my pillow. I cracked my eyes open, but quickly shut them for five more minutes of sleep. Each morning, my Mom would walk past my room to wake me then go down the hall to my brother Tim's room. I could always hear her footsteps coming back from Tim's room for her second round of wake-up.

"Annie, now."

"I'm up, I'm up.."

I threw the covers to the floor and rolled out of bed. I walked into my bathroom and grabbed my toothbrush out of the holder. The edge of the handle of the brush got stuck and my holder crashed into the sink and broke. I cursed to myself.

"Annie, what happened?"

"Nothing. I'm fine," I growled back.

I cleaned up the glass and I looked in the mirror. I noticed a red blemish just below my bottom lip. I touched it and it was tender, a pimple. I rolled my eyes and brushed my teeth.

I went downstairs to eat my breakfast. My stomach was churning and I thought I could hear a maniacal laugh coming from inside. I was hungry.

"Morning Annie," my Dad said with his usual chipper Friday attitude. "Oo, got a little sucker growing there under your lip!"

I put my hand up to my face and cringed at him. "Thanks," I replied. "Where are my Pop-Tarts?"

"Top shelf to the left. Need a bit of a pop this morning, do we?" He chuckled like a shopping mall Santa Claus. I shuffled past him to the cabinets.

I threw the cabinets open: Cheerios, Cocoa Puffs, Lucky Charms, no Pop-tarts. I blew my breath hard and slammed the cabinet shut.

"What's up your keester?"

"Forget it. I'm late for school. Bye." I grabbed a few Oreos and my book bag and stormed out of the kitchen.

It was the first Friday of the month, which meant we had Mass at school. After taking attendance, my class walked over to the church and we took our seats. The eighth graders walked in and Abby sat in the pew behind me.

"Hey, Fungus."

She hissed in my ear. Her friends giggled next to her. I remained silent, praying she would leave me be. I felt rage inside, stronger than my normal rage when she was around. I took a deep breath and settled myself. I couldn't overact in church. Mrs. Brindle told us if we even have a bad thought in church God will know. I only had bad thoughts about Abby, so I tried to think about something else. I didn't want to sign my permission slip to hell just yet.

Mass continued and it was time for Communion. My stomach had started cramping up around the homily, but I assumed I was getting hungry again. Oreos aren't the best breakfast. It was time for my row to go up. I was at the end of my row and Abby was at the beginning of hers, so she would be walking behind me in line.

Just before I stood up to walk into the aisle, I could feel it. The monster was excavating. It was like the feeling I get when I have to throw up but I couldn't hold this in. This had a mind of its own. I began to pray with every ounce of Catholicism I had in me. "God, if you are a true and good God do not let this happen to me right now."

God is mean.

I stood up. My stomach cramped from the movement. I could feel it. It trickled. I could do nothing, so I continued to walk. I got to the end of my row and I could hear the laughter behind me. It must have leaked onto my powder blue skirt. My cheeks flushed as Catholic guilt began to rise inside me. I remember hearing in religion class and in the video we watched that women are considered to be "unclean" when they go through their change. If it's so evil, why did God make us this way? What if the priest notices and has me sent outside? I wonder if the school has blood huts.

Suddenly, I felt a sweater being wrapped around my waist.

"Keep walking. You're fine."

I turned and it was Abby. She turned her head and made an "I will kill you face" at the other girls. There was immediate silence. Abby played it off as if I had dropped my sweater and she returned it to me. I processed up the aisle slowly as to not let the sweater slip. I hoped nobody noticed how weird I was acting. I got to the altar and I swear the priest knew.

"The body of Christ," he said, raising the host in front of me. And the blood of Annie, I thought to myself.

"Thank you," I said. He stared at me for a second. I shook my head. I swear I thought I heard him say, "Welcome to womanhood."

"Amen, I mean, amen." I threw the host in my mouth and blessed myself.

When Mass ended, I broke out of line to run to the bathroom. Mrs. Brindle called after me. Breaking out of line in Mass is equivalent to a venial sin. I ignored her though and continued running. I'd rather sit through eight detentions and risk going to hell for running out of line than continue to leak on my skirt. I turned the corner and there was Abby.

"Go ahead," I said to her, "say your worst. Looks like you had yourself an accident, Fungus. Clean yourself up Fungus, you're leaking." My hand started to shake, I thought I might slap her.

"Here," she said. She handed me a pad. I stared at it for a few seconds.

"Seriously?"

"Seriously."

I was shocked. How stereotypical for a miracle to occur in Church.

"You're not going to tease me? You're not going to shout to the whole school that my skirt is stained? Annie is bleeding everyone!"

"Come on, Annie, just take the damn thing before I change my mind."

I grabbed it from her. "You shouldn't swear in Church."

"Shut up. Now, do you know how to use it? Because I don't want to have to show you."

"Yeah, I got it."

"Good, I don't want to catch your fungus."

For the first time, I laughed at my nickname.

"Oh, when you get back to school, meet me in the girls bathroom on the second floor. I have a spare skirt."

"Okay."

She started to walk away.

"Hey, Abby. Thanks. You didn't have to do that."

"Sure I did. Welcome to the club."

3

Love Under the Monkey Bars

Connor Philips was the first boy I ever loved.

Some would say love is too strong of a word for a playground romance, but I was confident of how I felt when I was seven years old. I was emotionally advanced. I was one of the only ones who didn't believe in cooties.

Every day, my best friend Sally and I would sit in the sandbox after school. The playground was small, with one set of swings, a sandbox, a jungle gym, a slide, and the coveted monkey bars. It was our after school kingdom. There was a group of us whose moms couldn't pick us up right at 2:55 when the day ended, so we ruled the playground for an hour each day. The boys of the group ruled the monkey bars. A boy's reputation could be made or broken depending on his monkey bar skills.

Connor Philips was a monkey bar extraordinaire. The way I look at a shirtless David Beckham now, is the way I looked at Connor Philips then.

"Look at him swinging from bar to bar," I would say to Sally. "He looks like one of those spider monkeys, except cuter. You ever see those on the Discovery Channel?"

"Yeah I've seen them. They swing from trees and then throw poop on each other," Sally said.

"They don't throw poop on each other." I glared at her. I never understood the satisfaction she got from teasing me when I was in love.

"Sure they do. That's the brown stuff. Maybe Connor throws poop. You got to watch out for that. I heard he still wears pull-ups to bed at night."

She grinned as she stuck a stick on the top of her elaborate sandcastle. Nobody in our class wore pull-ups to bed at that age, especially Connor. I remember hearing he was potty trained at six months, he was advanced like I was. There was one kid, though, who wore pull-ups until fourth grade. Tommy Jones. He had a bladder problem. I remember nobody would sit behind him all the way through eighth grade. The older he got the worse it got. Everyone knew when he hit puberty because his farts started smelling worse.

"What? He would never throw poop." I flicked the stick off her sand fortress and the top part crumbled. She stuck her tongue at me.

"Well, I heard from Jimmy that he eats his boogers."

"That's not true," I said.

I looked down pretending to fix my sand castle, trying to hide the fact that I sometimes ate my boogers. If I didn't have a tissue, I didn't see anything wrong with it. Hell, I sometimes sneak a taste now when I'm alone. Who says we have to grow out of ALL of our child-like tendencies? It all goes to the same place anyway.

I remember when I first fell in love with Connor. It was in kindergarten. I sharpened his Forest Green crayon for him the first day of school. His favorite color was Forest Green. I was sitting in his quad in the desk across from him.

"You're getting dull," I said.

"Huh?"

"Your crayon."

"Oh, yeah. I really wish my Mom got me the box with the sharpener. I only have the twelve pack."

"Here," I said. With two hands I picked up my box and handed it to him.

"It has a sharpener and has seven different greens."

"Wow, thanks," he said.

The project he was working on ended up winning an award in the school-wide art show. I still take credit for that win.

Each month in our kingdom we held a monkey bars competition among our group. Only the boys were allowed to compete. There were eight boys split into groups of four. The boys rarely played with the girls because of course girls had cooties and boys were just disgusting. I didn't agree with that whole notion, but I followed the crowd. I didn't want to be banished from the playground kingdom. There was nothing worse than getting banished from the playground kingdom. One kid played with a girl and he was forced to take four spins on the merry go round thing then try to walk a straight line. He threw up his gold fish and had to go home early.

The girls would sit in the sandbox and watch as the boys competed. The only boy who spoke to the girls was Jimmy. Jimmy was like one of us, he enjoyed watching us do our hair and he loved to gossip.

"I'm going to beat him this time," Jimmy said one hazy May afternoon.

"Connor wins every month, Jimmy. You have no chance," I told him.

"You're a traitor Molly. Just because you have a crush on him doesn't mean you have to cheer for him. He has cooties anyway."

"He does not."

I folded my arms and walked back to my sandbox. I was putting the finishing touches on yet another masterpiece when Connor came over to my side of the playground to retrieve a ball that landed next to me.

"Oh hi Molly."

I froze, my hands knuckle deep in sand. "Hi."

"That's a neat sandcastle," he said bending down to pick up his ball.

I looked up at him. "Thanks."

"If you put some water on there it will stay better," he pointed to the needle I attempted to make at the top that kept falling over.

"My Dad taught me that at the beach."

I nodded. He grabbed his ball and walked away.

As soon as he was gone, Sally barreled towards me.

"He knows your name!"

"Of course he does, we've been friends all year."

"Please, sharpening a boy's crayon isn't how you become friends with him. It's not like you shared chips or something at lunch. A boy can get his crayon sharpened by any girl."

"Yeah, but sometimes a certain girl can be special. He's come back to me a few times to sharpen his crayon. That means I do it best."

I watched Connor go back to his side of the playground and saw his friend Steve yelling at him.

"Hey Connor, what do you think you're doing?"

"What do you mean?"

"You're friends with the enemy?"

"Enemy? It's Molly. She's nice."

"Doesn't matter Connor. She's a girl. I'm just reminding you of the rules you made." Steve shot a look at me. "Don't give her tips about making a sandcastle. You know about the sandcastle competition coming up in two months. We can't afford to lose again this year."

Connor shook his head. "You're right, Steve."

"Just don't talk to them. If your ball goes over there, send Ben to get it from now on. I can't risk you getting sick before the big competition."

For the next few days leading up to the competition, Connor wouldn't talk to me. He never really talked to me that much to begin with, but now he was being just plain rude. He let his friends destroy my sandcastle, he laughed when Steve stuck gum in my hair, and anytime his ball came over to my side he would send one of the nerds to retrieve it.

"Was it something I did, Sally?"

"Probably. I'm sure he realized you have cooties."

"Very funny."

"Molly, you'd be going against every schoolyard rule just by talking to him. Why don't you like Jimmy? He likes you."

I looked over at the monkey bars. Jimmy quickly turned his head. He was staring at me...again. Jimmy was nice. He had short hair glasses and freckles. But Connor, Connor was beautiful.

"Hey, hey Molly. Check out this new move," Jimmy said.

Jimmy swung his legs over one of the bars and hung upside down.

"Look Molly. I'm upside down."

"That's great Jimmy." I looked away.

He smiled. His legs slipped and he fell on his head into the wood chips. His glasses bounced next to him. Everyone laughed.

"Jimmy is hopeless, Sally."

The day of the competition had finally come. It was a Thursday, 3:30 PM. Our moms would be arriving in half an hour. The winner of the competition would be the new king of the playground.

"Everyone gather round," Steve shouted.

All the boys gathered near the monkey bars.

"Welcome to the monthly monkey bar competition. Today we have the defending champion, Connor."

Connor's friends cheered loudly.

"And Jimmy."

A few of Jimmy's friends cheered, they were mostly girls.

Three boys had already lost to Connor. It was finally Jimmy's turn to step up.

Steve laughed at him. Jimmy wasn't known as the strongest boy on the playground. He was the smartest, he knew his colors, shapes, and animals like the back of his hand. He even knew most of the Presidents' names, but his arms were nothing more than twigs.

"Very well," Steve said. "This month's competition will take place on the big kids' monkey bars. As always, the competitor will be timed. The best time wins and the winner becomes the king of our kingdom."

The groups made a collective gasp. Whispers were passed around like Starbursts. The big kids' monkey bars had 35 bars and were higher off the ground than the little kids' bars.

Jimmy's face went pale. He turned to the rest of the group.

"I can't do this. I can't do this. I've been practicing on our monkey bars. These are a completely different set of bars. We're not even allowed to go over there. I've never even see the big kids use those bars. What if they're broken, what if Steve made it so I have to fail. What if…"

Bobby grabbed Jimmy by the arms.

"Listen man, it's the bars. You love the bars. Doesn't matter what kind of bars they are, big kids, little kids. Be the monkey I know that you are."

"Jimmy, losers first please," Steve shouted.

Jimmy stepped up to the ladder that towered into the air. We all held our breath as he made his ascent. He reached the top.

"Jimmy. Jimmy. Jimmy." We began chanting, fists pumping in the air. A few of the squeamish girls shouted, "Oh, I can't watch!"

Connor's group howled in response. Jimmy stretched out his right arm and grabbed the first bar. Steve pressed start on his Pokémon stopwatch.

Jimmy moved like none of us had ever seen him move before, even swifter than Connor. His twig like arms moved so fast it was as if he was floating. He was nothing but a monkey bar apparition. Both groups went silent. He went from our side to the other in less than 15 seconds. He reached the other side and we erupted in cheers. He climbed down the ladder and ran to the embrace of his friends.

"Way to go Jimmy!" We all shouted giving him a group hug.

"Okay Connor," Steve said, patting Connor on the back. "You got this. He beat your record, but you got this. You were born for this. Remember back in preschool the first time you did the bars and you beat Donnie, who was two years older than you? You were the best and you still are the best. Do it for all the kids who can't do the bars. Do it for me, do it for you."

Connor nodded his head and climbed the ladder. He got to the top, took a deep breath and started swinging.

"Connor. Connor. Connor." His friends cheered as Connor flew. He was in spider monkey mode. As he neared the halfway point, the sun broke free of the clouds that concealed it and Connor was blinded long enough for him to miss the next bar. I watched as his fingers just barely grazed the 7th to last bar. He missed it, plummeting toward earth like a meteor, crashing into the wood chips, face first.

Nobody moved.

Connor lay motionless. I looked around me, but nobody attempted to go near him. I pushed my way through the crowd towards him.

"Connor, are you okay?"

He moved his arms to hoist himself up. His cheeks had red scratches across them and his upper lip was swollen. I could see tears silently falling. He sat there dejected under the monkey bars. I sat next to him and put my arm around him.

"Come on," I said, "let's go see the nurse."

Everyone gasped.

We walked to the nurse's office and she discovered that Connor had chipped his tooth. For the next few weeks, when Connor spoke he made a whistling sound. His family didn't have the money at the time to get his tooth fixed right away, so he was forced to walk around with a chipped tooth. His own friends made fun of him, even Steve.

One day after school, Connor came and sat in my sandbox.

"Molly, thanks for being my friend." His words whistled. "I've always liked you ever since you sharpened my Forest Green crayon."

"I like you too, Connor, but your friends think my friends have cooties."

"Well, let's change that."

He kissed me on the lips. I couldn't believe what was happening. I felt tingles in my toes and my shoulders shook.

"Connor!" Steve shouted across the playground.

"Look, Steve. I kissed a girl and I'm fine. No cooties."

Everyone gasped, unsure of what to do.

Connor smiled at me and dug his hands into the sand and began building his own sandcastle. The other kids stood in awe.

"Connor, what are you doing?" Steve shouted from the swings.

"I'm building a sandcastle Steve."

"But, but you're playing with the enemy."

Some of the other boys pushed passed Steve and joined Connor and all the girls in the sandbox. Steve stood alone watching, not sure what to do.

"This is crazy you guys. What are all of you doing?"

After realizing nobody would play with him, Steve walked over to a game of catch that included Sally.

"Can I play?" He asked, his voice nervous.

Everyone stared at him. He lowered his head and was about to walk away when Sally tossed him the ball.

"Of course." She smiled.

4

First Lust

I watch you as you stare at me.

It's the kind of stare that lures me in like a fish hooked on a line. You not only make me want you, you inspire in me an overwhelming desire to need you. Call it lust, call it love, but I can't take one step, one breath without having you.

It's the same stare that lured me in when we first met. We connected on a level I didn't know I could reach. I was younger when we met, so naive and unsure of how you could make me feel. I saw you through a window at the shop around the corner from my house. It was the same corner I came around every day. I had never noticed you before. It may have been that I was never looking for you, until that day. The sun reflected off the glass of the main window just as I was rounding the corner. It blinded my eyes. I closed them and raised my hand to cover the sun. I turned my head to the right and opened my eyes and there you were.

The sun shifted from my eyes to where you were sitting, a spotlight leading me to a new life. A life I had only dreamed about, a life that would be sweeter than my current one.

I still wish I had made my move then, but I knew I was too young to have you, too inexperienced; at least that's what my parents would have said. My parents would never have approved of such a relationship. Growing up, I watched very little television and never played games, not even card games because my father thought it encouraged gambling. Relationships were completely out of the question as well. I was to be protected and saved. When I saw you, I discovered my inner desire to want more, to be bad, to do things that would shock others. I felt things inside me that I had never felt. Tingles in places where I didn't know I could get tingles. I felt like a woman, sensual and liberated. One look at you had allowed me to release my inhibitions and come into my own.

I walked towards the window and placed my hands against the glass. I inched my face closer creating a little wet circle with the air heaving in and out of my nose. I started salivating in a way that startled me. I coughed nearly choking. I stood there, unable to comprehend the new sensations building inside of me. Part of me wanted to go formally meet you, to take you away with me and make you a secret part of my life. I wanted to make you a slave of my desires. I stood there watching you, until others began to stare. I slid myself away from the window and continued walking. I left determined to find you one day when the time was right.

Here I am now, staring you down again, like no time has passed at all. It's nothing like the old, familiar stare though. It's changed as our relationship has grown.

This time I'm older, wiser. I'm more sure of my taste. I know what I want, what I need, and what I'm capable of. You're in my possession and I make my own rules. I reach out tracing my fingertips along your smooth edges. I close my eyes, rubbing my tongue along my glossed lips. I inch closer to you and put you in my hand. Your soft texture warms my palm.

You melt, leaving remnants of yourself on my fingertips. I begin to salivate. I love it when I make you melt for me. I open my eyes and grin at you. I lift you to my mouth. My shoulders rise and my knees buckle. I wrap my lips around you and I take a bite.

The taste of chocolate and peanut butter explodes in my mouth creating an otherworldly sensation, a sensation I can finally enjoy whenever I choose.

Oh, Reese's peanut butter cup, my first lust.

5

First Kiss

Tim opens the door for me and I stumble out of the car. I wore heels and I don't do too well in heels, but I wanted to look good. As I step out, the heel of my left shoe gets caught on part of the seat and he grabs my hand to help me.
"Thanks."
I blush.
He grins back.
"Of course."
I hope he can't tell that my hands are clammy; they get clammy and sweaty when I'm nervous. I know it's unattractive, but I didn't have a chance to wipe them on my skirt before I got out of the car. Sweating is natural, he has to know that. He doesn't seem to notice though. His eyes are on my chest. I'm hoping it's because he likes the way I'm built and not because I have some gross stain on my shirt.

I just ate sushi and I ate it with chopsticks. I'm not too skilled with chopsticks. I've never really eaten sushi before for that matter, but I didn't want to get a big piece of meat and have him think I'm some carnivorous monster. I also didn't want to get a salad and have him think I'm a girl who's afraid of eating real food in front of other people. Plus, sushi seems sophisticated.

As he turns toward the house, I look down to check my blouse for stains or stray pieces of fish, nothing. He was just staring at my chest. I did buy a new push-up bra for this occasion.

He walks me to the door, holding my hand. The distance is about ten feet, but it's the most pleasant ten feet I've ever walked. He has nice hands, strong, but soft. I wonder if he uses moisturizer. What if he thinks my hands aren't soft? I haven't moisturized in a few days. What if he thinks I have man-hands; they are kind of big. Well, not really big, but they aren't dainty. What if he only likes girls with dainty hands? I can't stand those girls that have tiny hands and their ring size is the same as it was the day they were born. My ring size is an eight, but I'll just keep that to myself for now. It's not like he'll be giving me a ring or anything anytime soon. But, if it comes to that, I do know my size.

We get to the doorstep- this is it, the moment. Now is the time to bring out my A game. My A game has been out of commission so long I don't know if I can find it. My best move is staring at him while my mouth hangs open like I'm looking at a freshly made blueberry pie, my favorite. I lick my lips. Mm, blueberry.

"I had a great time." His smile widens.

"Me too."

I attempt to keep my voice at an acceptable level. I try to make it a whisper, a lady-like sensual whisper. It comes out more as a little-kid shout type whisper. He laughs. At least he's laughing. But is he laughing at me or with me? I laugh too because it seems to be the appropriate thing to do. We continue to stand there like two awkward turtles. He looks down at his shoes as if the answer to the question "What's next?" were lying within the laces of his Chuck Taylor's. He looks as nervous as I feel. He's holding both my hands now. His hands are clammy too.

"We should definitely do this again soon. I really like you."

Not only does he like me, he REALLY likes me. He wouldn't say it unless he meant it. Guys typically don't say things they don't mean. They aren't like girls. Their minds are simpler. I won't tell him that of course.

"I would love to do this again. I really like you too."

Wait, I said love. He only said we should do it again, he didn't say he'd LOVE to do it. Maybe he didn't notice I said love. He's grinning. I don't think he heard it. You can't say love on the first date.

He looks down at the ground again, shifting his sneakers against the pavement. I focus on his lips and perfectly quaffed dark brown hair. I want to speak, but I know whatever comes to mind will be a failure. I've been known to ruin a moment or two. I suppose it's best he finds that out sooner rather than later. It's silent again and we continue staring. He moves in closer.

My heart is thumping and I can feel my palms leaking an exorbitant amount of sweat. He's going to think I have a perspiration problem. I start salivating a little bit. I don't know if that's normal. What if he kisses me and my mouth is full of spit and I don't have time to swallow it before he makes his move? It would be like kissing a running faucet. Drool would drip out of my mouth and flow on to his chin. He'd be forced to jump back in disgust. Then he'd think I'm a bad kisser, which I'm not, but I could be better if I had practice. I've only ever kissed three guys.

My first was Tommy in third grade. He pecked me on the lips behind the swing set in the schoolyard.

I had a cold that day and had just finished blowing my nose before he kissed me. One stray booger clung to the edge of my nose blowing in the wind like a flag on a flagpole. He called me Booger Face until fifth grade.

Then there was Ben in eighth grade. We dated for a few days. On the bus ride home from a class trip, he tried to French kiss me with a mouth full of French fries. I don't think he understood the term French kiss.

Finally, there was Chris in tenth grade. We went out three times. On our third date, he French kissed me properly and also felt me up. It was the first time anyone other than myself had touched me there. His hands were so cold on my chest that I got startled and bit his tongue. I wouldn't wish a bloody French kiss on anyone.

Here I am now, a senior in high school. What if he thinks I'm a prude because I've only kissed three other guys? Well, he didn't ask me how many I've kissed and he shouldn't want to know. And they weren't really real kisses anyway. But he might ask if we continue to date. The question is, will we continue to date? I would definitely go out with him again, but does he want to go out with me? I can never tell what they're thinking, if they're thinking at all. He seems like a nice guy, but it's like my Mom always says, "They're all real nice until their pants start acting up." I guess he likes me well enough considering he asked me out. Boys just don't ask girls out for no reason, do they?

These thoughts swim through my mind as he inches closer. He lets go of my hands, puts his arms around my waist and pulls me in, like two magnets being drawn together. I lift my shaking arms and wrap them around his neck. He cocks his head to the side and leans in toward me. I follow the motions and tilt my head; he closes his eyes and I close mine.

Just as I'm leaning in to meet him halfway, an awful feeling rises from my stomach to my esophagus.

Oh no.

The taste of sushi resurfaces on my tongue. It feels like little invisible people crawling up my throat, grabbing my taste buds as footholds. I hold my breath for a second to block the explosion that's building up. I contract my stomach and try to close my throat to hold it in. I arch my shoulders back and stand rigid. His eyes are still closed, so I contort my lips to hold back my breath, making a fish face.

Not right now. Please, not right now. This cannot happen.

He leans forward. I can feel my face growing hotter, not from blushing due to the excitement of kissing a handsome boy, but from holding back a toxic bomb. I put my hands up to push him away, but I'm too slow. Our lips touch and then...I burp. I burp directly into his mouth. A billowing cloud of gaseous sushi breath is transferred from my mouth to his. A slight growl follows the cloud. The growl sounds like a dragon feasting on a Viking. He steps backward towards the bushes, bending over, wiping his face and coughing. I am appalled at my inability to control my bodily functions. I move my tongue around my mouth disgusted with the taste that has now materialized. I try hard to hold back the tears that are welling up in my eyes. Not sure if the tears are from embarrassment or from the raw stench of sushi.

He coughs into his hand and rubs his nose.

"Oh my God, I'm so sorry. That was so disgusting. It came out of nowhere just as you went to kiss me and I tried so hard to hold it in but I was concentrating on not missing your lips. I don't ever eat sushi, but I didn't want to get any meat or anything and tear at it like an animal. I can get out of hand when I eat steak sometimes. I thought sushi would seem sophisticated, but I have this thing with fishy foods and they don't mix with my stomach but I thought well maybe I'll try it. I did take some Pepcid beforehand to settle my stomach, but I guess that doesn't work for fish. And you ordered sushi so I figured I'd go for it. I didn't want to seem boring. I'm SO sorry."

Everything flows out of my mouth as quickly as the gaseous sushi burp. I speak so fast I'm not sure if he processes all of it. I bury my face in my hands, wanting to fall to the ground and disappear. I separate my fingers and look through the cracks like I do when watching a scary movie; unfortunately this horror story is happening in real time.

"I uh, I think I'm going to head out," he says turning towards the steps, holding back laughter as he shoves his hands in his pockets.

"I'm so sorry I ruined this."

"You didn't ruin anything. You have a good night. I'll call you soon."

He pats me on the shoulder, but it isn't a lover's pat of passion, more of a, "I feel bad for you," pat on the shoulder, a "see you later old chum" or "good effort" sort of pat.

I'm unable to utter any words as I watch him drive away.

I walk into my house, holding in the inevitable tears and the remaining gas still built up in my stomach. Thankfully, my parents are asleep. I go to the upstairs bathroom to brush my teeth and rid my mouth of the taste of sushi and failure.

It's the next morning. I leave the house before my parents can see me. As I step out of the door and walk down the ten-foot path to my car, images of the night before flash through my mind. Not such a pleasant walk this time.

I get to school early and sit in the library hidden by piles of books. I read through some notes for my first period class. I get up to look for another book and spot Tim through a shelf. He's talking to Chris, my bloody French kiss. They became friends last year when Tim transferred to our school. I situate myself so I can hear them talking.

"So how was it with Betty last night?" Chris says to Tim.

I breathe in like a vacuum sucking up every bit of air I can fit in my lungs, and I hold it.

"It was great."

The gust of air I release is so strong the books on the shelf shift. It was great? What? Does he enjoy getting burped on?

"Dinner was fun. We went to that sushi place on Market Street. I don't even really like sushi, but she suggested it, so I thought I'd give it a shot. At the end, I walked her to the door, kissed her, told her I'd see her again soon and went home."

He doesn't even like sushi? Why, why did I suggest sushi?

"That's it?"

Yeah, that's it? He seems to be forgetting the worst part.

"Yeah, I mean it was a school night, so I didn't want to keep her up. It was fun."

"Wow."

"Why are you so surprised?"

"Dude, I warned you about her last year. She bit my damn tongue."

Chris sticks out his tongue to show Tim the scar my daggers supposedly made two years ago. It wasn't really a bite, it was more of a nibble.

"There's nothing there except remnants of your Fritos, get over it."

"I don't know man. You sure it went that well?"

"It was a great night. I'm going to call her later this week. She's a nice girl, not to mention pretty cute."

"Oh whatever. I still recommend she wear a mouth guard if you ever make out."

They both laugh and turn to go to another row of books. I scurry over to my table, so they don't see me. I grab my stuff and rush to my first class. This is turning out worse than I thought. He's keeping it to himself because he's so embarrassed he can't bear letting anyone else know what happened. He can't even tell one of his best friends. I've ruined this poor guy. I mean it was only a burp, everyone burps, but it was a sushi burp. It was like opening the door to a fish market. I think I even spit a few pieces into his mouth. Regurgitation may be acceptable among the avian population, but not with humans. I'd almost rather him tell everyone.

The day drags on and last period finally arrives. I decide to skip because I have it with him. I walk down the back hallway to exit through the side doors, the "skipper doors" everyone calls them. I turn the corner almost free and there he is, at the water fountain. He's probably still washing his mouth out.

"Hey, Betty."

I pretend I don't hear him and continue walking. If I don't look, he'll forget about me. Out of the corner of my eye, I see him raise his head from the fountain, water glistening on his chin. I cringe thinking of the drool I sprayed on him just hours before.

"Hey, Betty."

He walks up behind me and taps my shoulder just like he did last night before he abandoned me on my stoop of disgrace.

"Oh, hi." I turn to face him.

"I was going to call you after school. You want to go out again this Saturday? A movie or something?"

I furrow my brow. "Yeah, okay. Did Chris dare you to ask me out again?"

"What?"

"Tim, I heard Chris telling you about me in the library today. I'm not worth the time."

"He was just being funny. I think you're great."

"Did you hit your head recently? You do recall me burping in your face and/or possibly regurgitating my sushi into your mouth right?"

He starts to laugh.

"Well, of course I remember that. It was hilarious. Pretty gross, but it could happen to anyone. Your reaction was kind of cute."

Kind of cute? Well, in that case, maybe I'll fart on our next date.

He stuffs his hands in his pockets and shuffles his Chuck Taylor's against the tiled floor.

"I don't know why you want to give me a second chance."

"Betty, you're pretty, you're funny, we had a great time last night. I'm not going to judge you on one mistake."

"You were laughing when you left."

"Well, it was funny. I didn't know what else to do. I was nervous and you looked embarrassed so I thought the right thing to do was leave. I didn't want to linger around and make you keep explaining yourself."

"You didn't leave because you were utterly disgusted by me?"

"There's a reason I asked you out in the first place. You might not remember, but you helped me find my classes my first day here last year. I've been thinking about you ever since. And if I was disgusted by you, would I be here right now asking you out again?"

"I guess not. But you really don't understand how bad I suck at this, all of this and I'd rather just let you move on and I'd rather not get my hopes up because I'm not worth..."

Before I can say another word, his lips are on mine. His arms sink down around my waist and mine fit perfectly around his neck. Our hips touch. My lips move with his the way they're supposed to, in one swift sensual motion. I even tousle his hair with my fingertips. He pulls away. It takes me a minute to catch my breath. He smiles.

"Those other guys should have stuck around for the second kiss."

6

She'll Pay

He took me to a diner.
I ordered mozzarella sticks.
He said he won't be eating.
I sat there eating my mozzarella sticks.

He started to complain about his friends.
He complained a lot.
A booger clung to his nostril.
It moved when he breathed, but somehow hung on.

He always had junk hanging out of his nose.
How did I never notice that?
I didn't have the tenacity of that booger.
I couldn't hang on anymore.

The check came.
"She'll pay," he said.
"It's mozzarella sticks," I said.
"I didn't eat. So, it's on you."

"I'm going to do what that booger never could!" I shouted.

He and his booger stared at me confused.

"I'm leaving," I said.

I drove off into the sunset to find someone who would buy me mozzarella sticks.

7

The Cut

I step into the small building, large mirrors and a row of chairs to my right, towering shelves of shampoo and styling gels to my left.

I go to sit in a small plastic chair in the waiting area by the front desk. Piles of celebrity gossip magazines lay on a small table in the middle of the row of chairs. Two other women sit across from me. They both have long hair like mine, flowing below their shoulders. Their legs are crossed and their noses stuck in the magazines. Their eyes are frantically taking in all the news about Brad Pitt and Angelina Jolie's thirty-seven children. I can't understand why those kids are such big news. So they have a lot of kids, who cares? I reach for the magazine with a half-naked picture of Justin Timberlake on the cover when I hear a voice.

"I can take you over here."

I look up, a woman with hair longer than mine points to an empty chair. With slight trepidation, I make my way to the back.

"Thank you," I say.

I slip into a black leather chair and I lay my back into the sink to get my hair washed. I shut my eyes. Visions of a new life flash by my eyelids. This will be my last wash like this.

"All done," she says, tearing me from my brief nap. She drapes a towel over my shoulders.

I stand up and walk towards her station.

I sink into another black leather chair. The arms of the chair are cold to the touch like blocks of ice. I shiver as I make a groove in the worn leather.

She reaches in a drawer and produces a plastic drape that she puts around me. It feels and looks like a large trash bag. She wraps it around my neck and latches the Velcro. It's tight and confining. I shake my head left to right. My wet locks slap down my neck over the chair and plastic drape. I look at myself in the intimidating mirror. I run my hand through my hair one last time, lingering a little longer, letting the ends brush my fingertips.

"So, what are we doing here?"

The hairdresser looks at me. She has one hand on her hip while the other clutches the tool that will change my life forever. I focus in on her face in the mirror. Her jaw slaps up and down chewing a small piece of green gum. I think hard about what I'm about to do and who I am allowing to do it.

"HELLO?? What do you want me to do?"

"Right, sorry," I say.

I reach under the plastic drape and slip my hand into my jeans pocket. I pull out my phone to show her the photo of the look I want.

Deep breath. "This is what I want," I say.

She gasps. "You sure you want to do this??"

I am ready to release myself from the confines of unoriginality. I am ready to begin anew. Why wouldn't I be sure? Must a girl be so attached to her hair?

Society encourages conformity. Everywhere I go, I see long tails swishing back and forth behind heads. Even some men have ponytails. Long hair is the trend, and you are considered crazy if you don't follow it. People walking down the street looking like teams of horses trotting. Swish, swish, swish, their hair flows back and forth swatting flies as they walk. I have grown tired of my own horsetail swishing against any piece of clothing I wear. I have grown tired of catching my locks in my coat zippers and accidentally eating a piece of hair while trying to take a bite of a burger. I remember asking my teacher a few years ago, if she knew many women who didn't have hair below their shoulders. My teacher ignored me and told me to quiet down, treating my question as blasphemy.

I hadn't told anyone I knew that I was going to do this. I didn't want the opportunity for anyone to talk me out of it. I did mention months ago to my best friend that I wanted a change in my life. She told me to go shopping. I told her shopping could only satisfy me to a certain degree. New clothes get boring and, chances are, whatever I buy everyone else is already wearing. I even lied to my Mom. She asked where I was going today and I told her I was going to the library to read for a while.

I take a deep breath, sit up straight, and project my voice.

"Yes, I'm sure. Do it."

"Okay. Whatever you want. Let me tell you now, I don't think this is a good idea," she says.

"Just do it," I say.

"Alright." She chews her gum harder. I notice her eyes widen.

I watch her raise her hand with scissors the size of hedge clippers coming towards my hair. I hold my breath and close my eyes.

Snip.

I watch as my brown hair litters the white tile floor, creating a bird's nest. I watch a piece of my youth float to the floor.

Snip.

There goes the time I cut my bangs in kindergarten and I had to wear a headband for four months. My Mom thought I was nuts because my brothers had never tried to cut their own hair.

Snip.

There go all the morning arguments I had with my Mom about how I wanted to style my hair for school, so many hours of brushing and blow-drying.

Snip.

There goes the time my brother sucked my hair up in the vacuum cleaner while he was vacuuming the living room. He was grounded for three weeks.

Snip.

There goes the time I was cousin It from the Addams Family for Halloween.

Snip.

See you later all the allowance money I spent on hairbands, scrunchies, clips, and bobby pins.

Snip.

Bye, bye best hair award I got in tenth grade.

Snip.

I hear gasps and murmurs from the other women in the back of the salon. I let my eyes slide to the right, trying not to move my head. I see them peaking over their gossip magazines. I have become more interesting than the celebrity trash in Star Magazine. I ignore them and focus my eyes on my own face in the mirror.

I am transforming myself into a new me, a new age of different.

"Wait, stop," I say. I put my hands up from underneath the plastic drape.

"I'm not done," she says.

"I need a minute."

She backs away and stares at me.

I breathe in deeply again, holding back tears. I want to do this. I have to do this, but it's still hard. Half my head has short hair. The other half is still long. The left side is new. The right side is old. At this moment, I am a living dichotomy. I look at what I am going to become and I look at what I was.

"Good bye," I whisper to the right side of my head.

"What?" The hairdresser looks at me with wild eyes.

"You can continue," I say.

She goes to the other side and completes the look.

It's called a pixie cut. I feel magical, free, like I have a pair of wings and I could fly to the ends of the earth.

The stares follow me as I walk to the door.

I look back with a smirk. "It's just hair," I say. "It grows back."

I step out of the door into the sunshine ready to live my new life as a pixie.

8

Pending

Friend request pending.

Pending? Seriously? I friend requested him thirty-six hours, three minutes, and two seconds ago...approximately. There's no way he hasn't been on Facebook in thirty-six hours. I get curious as to what is going on after being off for three hours. Statistically speaking, the average person in society goes on their Facebook at least three times a day. And that's just the average person. Pete seems like an average guy, but in my eyes he's above average. Being above average would mean he checks his Facebook more often than the average person.

I personally go on every day, just to keep up on everything going on. If I'm busy, I'll only go on seven to ten times. If it's a slow day, I might check it ten to twenty times. It also depends if I have my phone on me because I can access it from my phone, which I typically do have my phone on me, but I don't always check Facebook because it eats up my data plan. I'll check it on my phone at appropriate times, like randomly between classes, or in the elevator when I want to avoid making awkward conversation with the people riding with me. Everyone pulls out phones on the elevator. There's nothing weirder than elevator banter with people you hardly know. It also depends on the time of day. I'll check it in the morning, sometimes in the afternoon, and when I'm done homework at night I'll meander around the site until I go to bed. Everybody does it.

I only check because I never know when an important message might come in or a networking opportunity could arise. I have to keep my eye out for these kinds of things. And obviously I go on to make more friends. That's the way people make friends now. Sure, you meet them in class, but how do you learn about them? Ask them questions in person? No, Facebook.

I've been on a lot the past few days because they've been slow days. I'm on break from school and haven't had much to do, which is why I friend requested him. We had become great friends by the end of the semester so it was natural that Facebook friendship would occur. I'm surprised it didn't happen sooner or that he didn't friend me first.

I met Pete in psychology class. I read on his profile that he's a business major, so he just took the course for the credits. I'm a psych major, so it was a requirement for me. He sat next to me in the back row. The first day I was walking to the back of the room and I tripped over his bag.

"Sorry," he said. "Are you okay?"

He helped me up off the floor.

"Yes, I'm fine," I said.

I stood there smiling unable to lift my feet to continue walking. I was cemented to the floor. His face looked so smooth, like it was begging to be touched. His teeth were straight, a little yellowed, but nothing that couldn't be fixed with a white strip. Thinking back now, it could be from all the coffee he drinks. One of his "likes" on his profile is Starbucks. Anyway, his hair was combed neatly atop his head. He wore khakis and a button down shirt. Later that day, I had discovered I cut my knee. I stained my favorite jeans with blood, but it was blood well shed.

"Okay, sorry again," he said.

He sat back down and I made my way around him and sat in the corner, one empty seat between us. The professor was droning on about chemical imbalances in the brain or something, but I could only think about the chemical balance between Pete and me.

We also went to a party together towards the end of fall semester. Well, we didn't go together exactly, but we hung out together. I never really went to any parties, but one morning in class he said I should go.

"I'm going to a party Friday, you in?" He said over his shoulder.

I blushed. "Yeah, of course, if you'll be there."

"Yeah, man I'm game," John said.

"Sweet, dude," Pete answered.

John sat behind me. It was obvious Pete was talking to both of us, but he didn't want to seem too forward by asking me directly, so he involved his friend in the conversation. He didn't want anyone to know he was crushing on me. From what I can gather from his Facebook, he likes to keep his feelings to himself. He rarely ever posts a status.

The girl who threw the party isn't really a close friend, but we're Facebook friends. I came across her page in the school network, mostly because she's connected to Pete, and I noticed she had a quote about living life to the fullest. I thought it was uncanny, because I have the same quote on my profile and it's pretty much my life motto, so I knew we would be good friends. I friend requested her immediately and she accepted within six hours. I figured Facebook friendship is enough of a friendship to go to a party. I saw the event posted on her wall. It wasn't private, which means she wants everyone there. Her name is Sally Anne. When I saw Pete at the party I went right up to him.

"Excuse me, Pete," I said. I tapped him on the shoulder.

He was wearing a gray sweater. It looked like J. Crew. I like J. Crew. It felt so soft, like Cuddles, my gray bunny I had when I was a toddler. Pete even had cute beady eyes.

"Yeah." He turned to face me.

"Hi, it's me, from psych class."

He looked at me confused.

"You know, Judy, we sit in the back together. I lent you my pen the other day."

It was raining the day I lent him the pen and it was muggy in the classroom. When he returned my pen, it was warm, like a spoon after you take it out of a hot cup of tea. My hand is still pulsating with heat. There is so much energy between us.

"Right. What's up?"

"Nothing much. I was just thinking you really remind me of my childhood bunny."

"Oh?"

I could feel all the color seep off of my face, like a painting being sprayed with water. My stomach gurgled. His red Solo cup creaked from the tight grip he now had. I quickly responded.

"But besides that, do you know where Sally Anne is? I'd like to thank her for hosting this."

"Not sure I know a Sally Anne."

How can he not know the girl who is throwing the party? Who shows up at a random party without knowing anybody?

"She's throwing this party. This is her apartment."

"Oh, you mean Alex?

"Right. Alex. That's what everyone calls her?" I laughed. "I'm one of her best friends. My nickname for her is Sally Anne. That's why it's her name on Facebook. I made it up. It's a girl thing."

We weren't best friends, but I couldn't let Pete know that I didn't even know my semi-close friend's real name. Apparently, her name was Alexandra, but she changed her Facebook name to Sally Anne, so people couldn't find her. That's ridiculous. Who wouldn't want to be found on Facebook? And it's not even close to her real name. How are you supposed to become proper friends with people if you're advertising the wrong name? I understand when people use their real first name and their middle name. Like my friend Shannon is Shannon Marie. That makes sense. But Sally Anne? That's nowhere near Alex. That is not the way to get more friends and it's obvious people's popularity is based on how many Facebook friends they have. That's just the natural path society is taking. I only have 299 right now, with one pending, but I plan on bumping that up to at least 400 by the end of the year. Pete has 700. Maybe if I have more friends Pete will accept my request. It's understandable that he doesn't want to be Facebook friends with someone who has fewer friends than he does. I'm sure he has a list of pending requests that he needs to go through. I'm positive when he sees mine he will click accept. And it won't be hard to know who I am because I have my real name posted. Judith Rose Matthews. Hm, I should probably change it to Judy. Nobody here knows me as Judith.

"Cool. I thought I knew all of Alex's friends. I guess not," he said.

"Well, you know you can't know everyone, big school and all. I don't always come to parties, that's probably why you haven't seen me, other than class."

"Yeah, that's probably it. I'm going to go check out the beer pong game over there."

"Awesome, yeah. I'll totally join you. I'll be right over. I'm just going to get a drink."

"Right."

I watched as he walked away. His feet go inward a little bit as he walks. Pigeon toed I think it's called. I was pigeon toed when I was younger, but I grew out of it. I should post that on my profile. Maybe he'll realize we're even more similar.

I read on his profile that his favorite drink was Jack and Coke, so I poured myself a Jack and Coke. I can't really handle Jack and I honestly have no desire to drink Coke, I'm more of a Pepsi person, but it's important to step outside of your comfort zone once and a while. I added it later to my profile in hopes he would notice and accept my request. I stood near him during the whole party sipping my Jack and Coke. He didn't want to talk, or stand too close, which was fine with me. Silence and distance can be good sometimes. A lot can be said between two people just by being in the same room interacting with others. I am fluent in body language. I noticed him talking to a girl who looked familiar. It was Alex.

"Hey, Sally Anne," I said.

She gave me a face like I had something hanging out of my nose. I hope she didn't see that picture that my best friend posted last week. I really did have something hanging out of my nose. She tagged me when I told her not to. But I have no shame, it's cool if people know the embarrassing side of me.

"Huh?"

"Lol," I said out loud. She stared.

"I mean, Alex. What's up? Great party."

"Do I know you?"

"Yeah, it's me Judy. Well, Judith. I'm sure you recognize me from Facebook. My name is Judith on Facebook. We became friends a few days ago. We have the same quote about living life to the fullest."

"Very cool." She went to turn away, but I grabbed her by the arm.

"Thanks so much for throwing the party."

"Sure thing. Enjoy yourself."

"I will, thanks. I'll be sure to post some pictures."

"Great," she said. She rolled her eyes and floated across the room. That's so Alex. On her Facebook, she is a fan of the Sarcasm page. She has such a good sense of humor.

I pulled out my phone and snapped a few pictures.

"Smile," I shouted to the beer pong table. A few people looked up.

One of them shouted, "Who are you?"

"Judith Rose Matthews. Find me on Facebook."

A few people started laughing, so I laughed with them. They were such a nice group. I finished my Jack and Coke and announced to everyone I had to leave. A few people waved at me.

"Bye everyone. I'll see you in class Pete," I said to him.

"Yeah, sure," he said.

When I got back to my dorm that night, I threw up for two hours. I realized then if Pete and I were going to be together, I really needed to train myself to drink Jack. According to Sally Anne's Facebook, she was going to be throwing a few more parties during the spring semester, so I had plenty of opportunities to build up my tolerance. I was happy I held it in until I made it back across campus to my dorm. Throwing up at a party would have been so embarrassing. And I didn't want my photo ending up on Facebook. I heard this one group of guys makes a rule at each of their parties, if you throw up or pass out someone will take a picture and post it online. I would never want Pete to see me throwing up, whether it's in person or in a photo.

I posted the pictures on my profile the day after the party. I wanted to share every great experience with the world. I friend requested everyone so I could tag them. At least the people I could find. I found most of them through Sally Anne's/Alex's page. I don't have many tagged photos. If I go to more of Alex's parties, I'll definitely increase my number. I only have about 130. They're mostly from family outings. I don't want anyone thinking I only go to family parties. It's kind of embarrassing being tagged by my Mom.

Friend request pending.

It's now been sixty hours since Pete has been on Facebook. Maybe he doesn't have Internet access at home. That would be a nightmare. How does he handle not having Internet access? I can't even imagine what I would do. Maybe he's hurt. I know he was going skiing. I saw on Sally Anne's Facebook that she was going skiing with him. I wonder if they date? Her relationship status says single, so they probably don't date. Pete's status says unknown, again he likes to hide his feelings. I'm sure if there was an option he'd put "crushing on Judy Rose."

I go to Pete's profile to see his tagged pictures. He has a limited profile for those who aren't his friends, so I can only see a couple of his albums. One is from family events. He's a family man, perfect. Two others are from parties. I scan the party pictures. Alex is tagged in quite a few of them. He has his arm around her in a couple, but boys always put their arms around girls, it doesn't necessarily mean they're dating and a few of the captions say "my best friend." They're just best friends. They probably gossip and watch movies together. At least I think that's what best friends do. I haven't necessarily ever had a best friend, let alone a best friend that's a guy. Unless you count Cuddles, but Cuddles and I couldn't exactly gossip. I did teach him to get me the newspaper.

Pete's wearing a Beatles t-shirt in a lot of his pictures. I never listen to the Beatles, but I do have an interest in British culture. I'll post it on my profile under music. I have a lot of Taylor Swift type artists on there, but I can hide that. He doesn't need to know my pop obsessions until we get to know each other more. His music list is very eclectic, very Indie. I typically don't go for Indie, but there's a first time for everything. I wonder since he likes Indie music if he likes Indian food. I like Indian food. I'll have to start reading up on the latest underground bands. We could go to concerts and be way ahead of all of the trends and eat Indian food like exotic travelers do.

Maybe I should message him just to make sure he's aware my request is there. I'll definitely message him. He probably hasn't seen the request yet. It's easy to overlook a friend request. He probably gets a lot per day so he doesn't respond to all of them right away.

Hey Pete, it's Jude, ha ha isn't it funny how shortening my name can be like the Beatles song?! I just wanted to let you know I friend requested you. I know you probably have a lot of requests, so I wanted to make sure you were aware of mine. Great party the other night at school. I had a lot of fun with you. It was great getting to know you better. We really have a lot in common. I hope your break is going well. I'm looking forward to many more great times.

-Judith, Judy, Jude

I think about signing it with "love, Judy," but that I'm sure I'll hear from him soon. I think I'll poke him too. Everyone loves a good poke war. He's bound to see the poke notification. I click the down arrow of the section where the poke button is.

Poke.

Okay, that's all I can do for now. I direct my mouse to the log out button. I search around the page clicking buttons. I rarely click the log out button, but I do when I am home on break. Last time I stayed logged in my older brother changed my status. "Judy is pooping." First off, girls don't poop. Second of all, if I did I would never tell the world about it.

Log out. I shut my laptop and lie down to go to sleep. I stare at the ceiling counting the glow-in-the dark stars on my ceiling from when I was young. I used to count them before I went to sleep to make sure I wasn't missing any. Still fourteen. I stare so hard at them they look as if they're ingrained in the ceiling. Maybe I should check just to make sure. No, I should go to sleep. A good night's sleep will help. I'll wake up and it'll be a new day. Even though it is already the new day, it's 1 AM.

My alarm goes off at 11 AM. I slam my hand down on the off button. I rub my tired eyes. I haven't been on Facebook in ten hours. I haven't done that, well, ever. Except for when I didn't have a Facebook. I don't like to think about those days. Those were dark times. I spent most of my time on AOL Instant Messenger. What a relic.

I run past my computer so as not to tempt myself. My parents already left for work, so I sit down at the kitchen table to eat cereal. I shovel the Cocoa Puffs into my mouth, my leg shakes, my hand twitches. I have to check. I run back upstairs to my room and throw open my laptop. I log in.

Friend request pending.

Still pending, no message in my inbox, and no poke return. He's playing hard to get.

The next day I go back to school. I don't have classes with Pete this semester. I made sure to check before break ended. I hacked into his student account to check his schedule. I just wanted to make sure, since I couldn't contact him to find out. I planned on running into him on my way to lunch. He listed on his profile which building he lives in. It happened to be one that is connected to mine through a common area. I wouldn't list where I live on my Facebook, but Pete is so confident and has such trust in his online friends that he gives out information like that. It's probably also a way for him to tell me. I know he's interested in me. It's obvious.

I wait in the common area, the school news drones on the TV in the background.

"Coming up next, Jill will tell us the new studies of the effects of social media on college aged students…"

I check my watch. 12:28. He typically gets to the cafeteria at 12:35 every day, which means he'll walk through the common area at 12:30.

12:30.

"Hey Jude," I shout as he walks into the common area.

He looks at me with his brow furrowed. He looks just like Cuddles.

"What?"

"Beatles reference," I say. "I hear you like the Beatles."

I was going to say I saw it on his Facebook, but I can't let him know I Facebook stalk him, even though everybody does it, but it's socially unacceptable to admit it.

"Oh, yeah. They're cool." He continues walking and I follow. I'm going to the cafeteria anyway.

"I just started getting into them. I read an article about Yoko Ono the other day. You know she's eighty years old now?"

"Wow, that's crazy. She's getting old."

"Yeah, it's really a shame she's been without John all this time. Do you think she was the reason they broke up?"

"Uh, I don't really know. Listen, I've got to run, I'm late meeting Alex for lunch."

"I'm going to lunch too, I'll walk with you."

"Oh, um, alright."

We talk the whole way there. Well, I talk. He listens. That's how it goes between us. A good listener is a good find. We get to his usual table and Alex is there.

"Hey Alex," I say.

"Oh, hey. Uh, sorry your name is?"

"Judy. I came to your party before break."

"Right. Good to see you."

"You too. I'm looking forward to more parties."

Alex turns to Pete.

"Hey, babe." She leans up and kisses him.

I stall in a mid sit/stand position. My butt sticking out and my chest facing downward towards the table. My fingers dig into the back of the chair.

They date.

I've spent all this time preparing myself for him and he dates Alex? It's not on Facebook. How am I supposed to know if someone is in a relationship if it's not on Facebook? If I were in a relationship, I would post it because there are so many eligible bachelors on Facebook who would be looking at my profile and trying to date me and they would know I'm not available by seeing the "in a relationship" sign. That's what it's for. I feel so completely stupid.

"I need to go. I forgot about something where I'm needed. Bye."

"Bye," they both say.

I turn my back to them to pack up my bag and I swear I hear her whisper to Pete.

"Who is that girl? She was all over you at my party."

"She's this girl from my psych class from last semester. She creeps me out. She friend requested me on Facebook. I need to block her," he says.

This girl from my psych class? That's all I am to him. We share so much and that's all I am to him. He's in denial. I'm not creepy, he just can't admit to his girlfriend who he really wants.

"Stay away from her. She's strange."

I run out of the cafeteria trying not to cry. It's only a matter of time until Pete figures out I'm who he wants. I hold it together for my final class of the day, English class. I walk to the back of the room, but I remember the last time I walked to the back of the room on the first day of a class I fell...in love.

After being scorned, I decide to try my luck in the middle of the room. I sit down, take out my notebook and realize I don't have a pen. I turn to the person next to me, or should I say the image of perfection next to me.

I swear lighting struck me between the eyes. His hair is a beautiful mess. His face is covered in stubble. His t-shirt is ripped, his jeans are ripped and he is wearing dark blue Converse sneakers. Converse. Sneakers. Heart melted.

"You're perfect," I say.

He turns his head towards me. As he turns, his hair flops to the right side.

"Excuse me?"

"I said do you have a pen?"

"Yeah, sure," he says.

He hands me a pen. The cap is a little chewed. All my pen caps are chewed.

"Thanks."

"Sure thing," he says.

"I'm Judy," I say. "Judith Rose Matthews."

I want to make sure to tell him my full Facebook name.

9

Mocha Frapp with Tears

Another Saturday in the office.

I don't know why I took this job. Mindless office work when I could be sleeping in my warm bed.

Oh wait, I know why I took it, because I don't have a job and I've spent too much time in my bed the past few months. Whoever said graduating from college was exciting was wrong. I couldn't be less excited. I was supposed to take four years to figure out what I wanted out of life, instead I ended up graduating with two things: an incredible tolerance for whiskey and the ability to unwrap a Starburst in my mouth in record time. I wasn't the most motivated individual, but I did get it all done. I studied communications. My dream is to be a news anchor.

Instead, for now, I'm here in a small office four days a week. The other three days of the week are spent contemplating the meaning of life, a.k.a. surfing the Internet for jobs, Facebook stalking my more successful friends, and playing Bejeweled. I have the first six high scores on the online board for Bejeweled. I battled a guy whose username was GamerMan1020 for three weeks for the number one position. It was a Wednesday when I surpassed his score and I screamed out loud in the office. It wasn't the first time I've screamed out loud during work. I'm more proud of my Bejeweled scores than I am of my college degree. I'm considering putting online-gaming as a skill on my resume, right next to sociable and works well with others.

The job isn't half bad. I sit and hand out pamphlets, answer phones, tell people how awesome my town is and eat left over donuts. It is mindless work, but it's money. Nobody ever comes in on a Saturday though.

My desk looks out on a big window. People will walk by to look at the window display and wave and smile at me. Sometimes I think about doing flips and cartwheels to entertain them and maybe they'll tip me. Then I realize my body won't let me do those things and I resort to looking back at them, waving and muttering through clenched teeth, "Please, let me out of here."

Lunchtime is always a relief. I take an hour and I walk up to Starbucks, get a Mocha Frappuccino and a piece of iced lemon pound cake. Not the healthiest meal, but it gives me the sugar rush I need to make it to five o'clock. If I end up being 500lbs within a year, maybe I could be on TLC.

I grab my sunglasses off the desk and lock up the office. I see a few people I know on the street, I wave and nod my head. I walk into Starbucks and join the long line of coffee drones.

"Hey Julie," Frank says, waving behind the counter. Frank is my favorite barista.

"Hey, Frank. The usual please."

"One Mocha Frapp with whip cream and a piece of iced lemon pound cake coming right up."

"Thanks, buddy."

I pay the cashier and wait behind the few people ahead of me to receive my drink. I take off my sunglasses and I notice a pair of eyes staring me down from the corner of the room.

Shit. It's him.

George.

George and I dated for eight months my senior year of college. We broke up just a few months ago in July. I would like to say it was mutual, but he dumped me. He said we were moving in different directions and I wasn't what he wanted anymore. I never thought I'd see him again. I knew he wasn't graduating on time and he was still in town, but I figured he would stay away from my favorite spots. He knew I lived for Starbucks.

It didn't end well, the George and Julie saga. Everyone on campus knew us as one unit. They even gave us a nickname like gossip magazines do to celebrity couples. They called us Georgie. It was cute at the time, now the thought of it makes me dry-heave. It's really not even that clever. George and I were a classic boy meets girl, boy likes girl, boy and girl date scenario. We had the same friends, most of the same classes. He wasn't traditionally handsome, but pleasing enough and I'm fairly pretty so it offset his awkwardness. The biggest difference between us was our morals; I had them and George didn't. George cheated on me with a girl from one of our classes, for four of the eight months we were together. I found out two days after we broke up. I don't know if I was more mad that he cheated or that I was so blind to the fact that it was going on. I feel even dumber that he dumped ME. I thought I had the upper hand in the relationship. I didn't even get the chance to find out he was cheating and dump him first.

When I look over, he looks right at me then looks down at his computer. I shake my head. Really? He knows I just saw him. Instead of making a scene, I pull out my phone and text him.

"Hey, I know you saw me.

I watch as he sees his phone light up. He looks at the screen and reads it, then looks up at me, looks back at the screen, and finally stands up. He shoves his phone in his pocket and walks over to me.

"Julie," he says.

"George," I say.

"You look..."

"Great? Yeah, I know I do. I've been working out." I say.

Lies. I've been eating iced lemon pound cake every other day and lying in bed after work. The most strenuous activity I do during the day is walking from town to home, which is 1.4 miles.

"Yeah, that's awesome. Great. I can't believe it's you," he said.

"And you, you look like death warmed up," I said.

His hands wrap around his stomach. His teeth gnaw at his lip. I remember he used to do that when he was nervous.

"Right, yeah. I'm not well. I, uh, heard you still live around here," he said.

"Yeah, I heard you still haven't graduated," I fired back.

I try not to be mean, but it's so easy.

"Yeah, you know, things have been hard for me since, well since..."

Before he can finish, his hand flies up to his mouth and he runs to the back of the room and slams the bathroom door. The coffee drones in front of me and behind me get a rush of caffeine from the scene. All eyes are on me. I stand there in shock.

Frank notices the commotion. "Everything okay, Julie?"

"Yeah, I'm fine. Can't say as much for that guy."

"Here's your mocha frapp," he says as he laughs.

"Thanks," I say.

Part of me wants to leave, but part of me wants to see what the hell he's going to say when he comes back out. I walk over to the love seats in the front and sit down. I bounce my left leg up and down on the ball of my foot. I sip on my drink, energizing myself with each sip. I wait a few minutes and then decide I should leave. I have no reason to hear anything he has to say. As I stand up, I see him walking towards me.

"Hey," he says.

"I'm leaving," I say.

"Please, just sit down for a minute."

His eyes are red and his whole body is shaking. I sit down for a pity talk.

"Listen, I'm not okay. I just threw up," he says.

Gross. He cries harder. I sit down and he sits down in the love seat next to me.

"Seriously, you threw up? And you're crying?"

"Julie, life has been horrible since we broke up. My Dad lost his job, I'm responsible for my little brother most of the time, I lost my part-time job, I have no friends anymore and school is harder than it has ever been. It all started going down hill when we broke up."

"You think I'm the reason your life sucks?"

"Please, I'm begging you. Take me back. Make it all better."

"Take you back? Really? One, you broke up with me. And two, I found out just two days after you dumped me that you were cheating on me with Patty. And three, the sight of me just made you vomit. Don't think it's meant to be,

George"

"Patty didn't mean anything, it's you I love."

"You were with her for four of the eight months you were with me, so she meant enough for you to lie to me for that long."

"I was being stupid and you weren't exactly there for me for a few months towards the end of school."

"There for you? I wasn't there for you?" My voice rises.

"Don't get loud please," he says.

"Oh, I'm going to get loud," I say. People start to look at me. "I was there for everything for you. I helped you get that part-time job at the radio station. I helped you get your grades back on track. In fact, my grades suffered a little bit because of you. I helped you make a name for yourself at school. You were nobody until you met me."

"And now I'm nobody without you. Please, let's go back to your place and talk about this," he said.

"That's your own fault. You can't play with people's feelings George. I really cared about you. I really wanted to make you happy, but you made me realize I can't please everyone. I need to think about myself more often and make myself happy. I have nothing I want to hear from you. The only thing I would want to hear is an apology, but you know what, that wouldn't mean anything to me. You're a liar and a manipulator. You think your life is going down hill because of me? Please, you're doing it to yourself."

I grab my bag and stand up. Everyone in Starbucks is staring at me. One girl starts clapping.

"Julie," Frank says, "I think you guys need to..."

"Don't worry Frank, I'm leaving." I turn to George. "Have a nice life."

George sits in the love seat and continues to cry. I walk out of Starbucks into a new perspective with a euphoric happiness surging through me. I spent months wondering what I had done to make him want to cheat, wondering why I wasn't good enough. It is him who isn't good enough. I walk back to my office with my head high. I smile at his misfortunes as I enjoy my mocha frapp with tears.

10

His Roommate Walter

He told me he loved me on date three.
So I said it back to be polite.
I didn't exactly mean it,
But I didn't want to start a fight.

We went on lots of dates,
He paid for all of my food.
I had never been so well fed.
I thought maybe I really did love the dude.

He called me many times a day,
Which seemed a little much.
But he had very nice hands.
I thoroughly enjoyed his touch.

He was enamored with me.
That was a perk, it's true.
He hung on every word I said,
And did everything that I told him to do.

One thing I did wonder about,

HIS ROOMMATE WALTER

Was his closet that was always locked.
Everyone needs privacy.
I wasn't all that shocked.

Until one day I saw the door ajar,
I just had to check it out.
I saw a sculpture of my head
With candles strewn about.

I asked him what it was
And he said it was his altar.
He prayed to my sculpture every night.
He and his roommate Walter.

I didn't realize he had a roommate.
He told me he lived alone.
I told him I can't date a man with a roommate.
And, I was taking the sculpture home.

11

A Text Message

"I'll text you tomorrow, gorgeous."

That's what he said last night, Saturday, when he dropped me off. I'm almost positive he called me gorgeous. If he didn't say gorgeous then he definitely said beautiful, one of the two. It doesn't really matter what he said, the general consensus is he likes my face. He smiled when he said it, it was right after he kissed me on the cheek. My cheek is still glowing red like I was slapped, love slapped. It was our first date and it was, for lack of a greater word, "majestic." We only went to a pizza shop around the corner, but it was the most perfect pizza shop my eyes have ever seen, mostly because I was sitting face-to-face with him.

We met a few weeks ago at a concert. A fight broke out in the crowd right near where I was standing. I nearly got hit, that's when he stepped in and pulled me from harm.

"I've got you beautiful, don't worry," he said as he scooped me up into his arms. He said something like that. He definitely said, "I've got you."

I asked him for his number by the end of the night. I know that's not exactly male and female protocol, but who follows rules anymore? I see nothing wrong with a girl asking a boy for his number. I texted him right after we parted ways, a girl has to make sure she wasn't given a fake number.

"Hey, it's me."

"Hey, sorry, who?"

He was so funny. Pretending he didn't know who was texting him, that's so him.

"You know, Jen from the concert. Call me sometime."

"Hey yeah, for sure. Nice meeting you."

That was our first text conversation. I have it saved in my phone and I revisit it often. What a wonderful conversation it was. It was so simple, but so complex if you really study the subtext of the text. "Nice meeting you" could translate to "It's nice that I've finally found you."

It's Sunday now. He said he would text me in the afternoon. Well, he didn't say afternoon, but when he said I'll text you tomorrow I can only assume he meant the afternoon. I wouldn't expect him to text me on a Sunday morning. Who texts on a Sunday morning? Well, I do. I text anytime of day really- morning, noon, or night, but he may not be like that. He may not want to seem too desperate or want to disturb my sleep. That's so kind of him.

I wouldn't want to disturb him either. Being a young man who goes to school and works all week, he probably enjoys sleeping in on a Sunday. He's in college and works downtown. I don't really remember what he said he studies or what his job entails. He went on and on about it, but I was fixated on watching his lips move. I noticed how the right side of his face curls up when he smirks and his head tilts slightly to the side that his face is curling. He also cracks his knuckles a lot while he's speaking, probably a nervous habit. I have the same one.

The only part I remember about his job is he interns at an important office and he wears a suit. What a man. I bet he looks good in a suit. His broad shoulders would fit nicely in a jacket. I can't wait to go out to a fancy dinner with him and wear his jacket when I get chilly on our walk home. I just know he'll be that guy.

I, being a young woman, need to catch up on my beauty sleep after a night out with a dapper gentleman such as him, so I wouldn't want to be awakened by a text message early in the morning. It's been proven teenagers need more sleep than infants. Even though I did get up rather early this morning, 8:00 a.m., early for me at least. I couldn't sleep from all the excitement of last night. He's just wonderful! I could even go as far as saying he's perfect, perfect for me.

I do wonder why he didn't say he'd call me. Is calling passé now? I suppose it is. My own mother and father don't call me anymore, they text me.

"Hey sweetie! I just watched the Ellen Show it made me lol. -Mom"

"J, can you pick up trash bags at the market? Thanks. –D"

I don't know what's more frightening: that they text or that they both use lol.

Texting is the new thing with everyone and I want to keep up with the new things. I'm typically behind on trends. There was a trend at school where everyone wore bracelets made from Starburst candy wrappers. I went home and took weeks to construct the greatest candy wrapper necklace, only to come to school and realize I was three weeks late on the trend. Everyone had moved on to bracelets and necklaces with bottle caps. But he doesn't need to know that.

I don't want him thinking I'm old school and want to blab to him about my girl-gossip over the phone and use up all his weekend minutes. I know boys don't like hearing about girl-gossip. And he's in college, so he's probably trying to save money. I don't want to be annoying right off the bat. I'll wait a little longer for him to find my annoying side, which of course I don't really have.

Phone calls will be appropriate when we've been going out longer, like a few months. We technically haven't been dating very long, considering we've only gone on one date. However, it could be argued that the night we met was a date since we spent the evening together after he saved me. I'm assuming we're an item, but it's not like he's exactly asked me to be his girlfriend. I'm not even sure they do that anymore.

The last guy I dated just called me his "shorty." I never really understood that nickname considering I'm average height. He just did it to seem more "gangster" I guess. I met him outside of a convenience store.

I ended it over text message after a few weeks.

"This isn't working anymore. I can't be your shorty."

"Okay, peace."

That was pretty harsh. Pretty sure there's a song about how you don't text message break up, but he didn't seem to be affected by it. The relationship, if I can even call it that, only lasted four weeks. I didn't follow any dating rules with him, so maybe I should follow rules with this guy. Well, if I'm following rules then I've already broken two by getting his number and texting him first. I don't have to count those two times.

I guess texting me is better than Facebook messaging me, or even worse tweeting at me. That's so indirect and not as intimate as a text message. Facebook is all about telling everyone everything. I wonder if we'll go "Facebook official" after he officially asks me face-to-face to be his girlfriend. Will he want it to be on Facebook? I wouldn't mind posting it on the Internet. My philosophy is to share life with everyone. Some people do say if it's not on Facebook it's not real, but I don't want to be one of those people and he doesn't seem the type. If he wants to though, I'll do it. I'd like people to see who my boyfriend is.

I must admit that I did tweet about him the night we met.

"Met my dream guy tonight."

He can't see it though, because he doesn't follow me... yet. He probably doesn't have a Twitter anyway and maybe it would be best if he didn't. He's a college man, much too sophisticated for a Twitter.

I check my phone again after not looking for twenty minutes. I need to make sure the sound is turned up. Yes, volume is all the way up and his ringtone is set. I have a special ringtone for him, but I didn't tell him that because that might scare him. It's that song, "You Make My Dreams Come True" by Hall & Oates. What a classic song. I wonder if he likes Hall & Oates. So far he has made my dreams come true. I mean rescuing me in a crowd of people is something out of a dream.

I don't want to tell him that though, then he might start having nightmares about me and I don't want to be a nightmare to him. I want to make his dreams come true too. I want to be the one person he can tell everything. Only me though, he won't need anybody else when he has me.

I would text him, but after texting him the first time immediately following the concert, my friends warned me to never do it again. They say I have to let him text me. Men are hunters; they enjoy the chase. I don't agree with that because how is he supposed to know I'm interested if I don't contact him? How is he supposed to know to like me back if he doesn't know if I like him?

What was that? I heard a noise. I check my phone. Nope. Nothing. Sometimes, when I'm waiting for a call or text I think I hear it go off. I'll just leave it in my bedroom and go downstairs for a while. Occupying my mind with something else will make the time go faster. I'll go on the computer and check Facebook. That always occupies at least an hour or three of my time. We became Facebook friends the day after we met. I'm a little ashamed to admit I found him and friend requested him first, but he accepted just 22 hours later, I think that's a sign. He didn't have to accept my friend request; he could have easily denied it.

He could have started a poke war with me, although, it may be too early in our relationship to poke. I don't want to rush anything, taking it slow is a good idea. I'm sure he believes that too. I'm sure we'll poke somewhere down the line. He also could have written on my wall or put me in his status, "I had the greatest night of my life with the best girl I've ever met!" That would be a flattering status. Let's see, here's his page.

"Billy is tired."

Why would he want people to know he's tired? Maybe that's code for, "I had a great night last night." That's got to be it. People are constantly writing encrypted messages as their Facebook statuses. Aw, his profile picture is so cute. It's him with his little sister at a family Christmas party. At least it looks like it's a family Christmas party and I'm guessing she's his little sister. There's a Christmas tree behind them and presents, and it looks like old people sitting on a sofa to the left, probably his grandparents. They look like such nice people. They're smiling without even knowing they're in the picture. They must be happy together. I can't wait to take a picture like that with him. I just know once our relationship progresses we're going to have so many pictures of us on Facebook. If he's from a happy family that means he's a happy guy, which means we'll be happy.

I can see the two of us walking down the street with our arms wrapped around each other's backs.

"Jen, a senior in high school, walking with a college man?"

That's what the girls at school will say. I'll just smile and nod, looking forward to so many beautiful days ahead of us. I'll go to all of his college parties and formals and he'll tell all his friends, "This is the one." Many girls will hit on him, but he'll scowl at them like the animals they are, and come home to me. When we both graduate, from the same college of course, we'll move away to the beach to start a family. He'll be a successful business owner. I prefer a man who can be his own boss. Meanwhile, I will be home with the children, while maintaining my clothing business, Jenny's Jumpers. We'll have six children, three boys and three girls, just to be even. Oh they'll be the most brilliant looking children. They'll have his dark hair and chiseled features with my hazel eyes, genetic jackpot. He has a few pictures of himself on Facebook as a child, what a cute child he was. I was a pretty cute child so it's only natural that we would produce the best looking children.

I'll just scroll down and see what kind of friends he has. Hmm, a lot of girls have written on his wall; I wonder if I have fierce competition. One of them said, "Great party the other night." Did he have a party? If she said the other night that means it was recent like this past week, possibly Friday. That's why he couldn't go out Friday. I specifically requested we go out on Friday to allow him to take me out again on Saturday.

That's okay if he had a party and didn't invite me. We're not official yet after all, at least official enough where he is required to bring me everywhere. Plus, I was busy on Friday night. I had to dog-sit, so there. I couldn't have gone anyway.

"Hey I'm throwing a party and it'd be awesome if you could come."

"Sorry, I have a previous engagement, thank you for the offer."

He also could have gone to a friend's party and didn't want to reveal me just yet. That's understandable. He wants to wait for the perfect moment to reveal his new love interest. That's a big deal and I appreciate him waiting. I'm sure I was a major topic of conversation at that party.

I'll just click "view friendship" to see if he responded to her wall post. Nope, just what I thought, he didn't respond. Sorry Sally, Billy is all mine. Her profile picture is of her doing a keg stand. How UN-lady like. I would never make that my profile picture, or do a keg stand at all, unless of course Billy asked me to do one. I trust that he knows what's right for me.

I'm going to check my phone again. It's half past noon. He's got to be awake by now. No messages. Maybe my phone doesn't have good service. I'll stick it in the window. Sometimes if I set it in the window the service increases. I'll bring it downstairs and place it in the window while I make some lunch. He's probably getting a shower, that's a good sign. Good hygiene is an admirable trait in a young man. Last night he smelled like my two favorite things, oranges and chocolate. I have no idea what cologne it was, but the scent is still lingering in my nostrils.

I'll turn on the TV for a little bit while I eat. HBO usually plays some good movies on a Sunday afternoon. Let's see, channel 301. *He's Just Not That Into You*. This movie is filled with neurotic people who don't know what they're doing when it comes to love. Maybe he hasn't texted me because he isn't that into me. I am sort of acting like that one girl in the movie who freaks out over all the guys by obsessing over every little detail. She even goes as far as "accidentally" bumping into them. I wouldn't do that. But she is the one who ends up with the guy at the end, so even if I am similar to her I will end up with Billy. I'm much cooler and calmer about all of this than she is though, but then does that mean I won't end up with him? I really don't care all that much if he texts me. There are over six billion people on the planet and probably half of them are men and millions of those live within at least a hundred miles of me, so chances are I'll meet at least one of them.

"And how, I can't explain. But you make my dreams come true."

There it is! I jump off the sofa and run to the window. It's him. I grab my phone and stare until my eyes burn. My hand turns white from clutching so hard.

"Billy: Text Message."

I run up the stairs to my bedroom. I have to be in my room when I open it. It's important where you're sitting when you receive a text message from a male, especially a new male. It's such a nice memory to look back on when you've been together for a long time.

"Ah yes, I remember where I was when I received one of the first text messages from your father, children." I'll probably have to explain to them what a text message is. By then, they'll probably have hologram messages.

I almost don't want to open it. Oh I can only imagine what it says. "Hey beautiful, last night was great. What are you doing today? I can think of nothing better than spending more time with you." Yes, that's definitely what it says.

I throw my stuffed animals off my bed and sit down. I prop up the pillows behind my back to get comfortable. There really is nothing worse than sitting in an uncomfortable position when you're texting. We could be texting for hours or maybe he'll even call me after we text! Here it goes. I slide my finger across the screen, the message pops open.

"Hey. How are you today?"

What a great word hey is. It's just sublime, is what it is. And he asked me how I am. It blows me away how considerate he is. There is nothing more considerate than asking a girl how she is. I could go on for hours telling him how I am and how I've been thinking about him since the moment I left his side and how I want to do nothing more than gaze into his eyes for hours telling him about my hopes and dreams.

I look up from my phone and breathe a sigh of relief. I close the text message and toss my phone on my bed. I'll text him back soon. I don't want to seem too desperate.

12

One More

"Hi," he says to me as I swivel around on the bar stool, trying to counteract the spinning of the world.

"Hello," I say in return, letting the **o** drag on a little longer than necessary. I slow my swivel and turn to the left to face him, but there's nobody next to me.

"Over here," he says.

I swivel to my right and there he is sitting on the bar.

"Why are you up there?" I blink a few times to hydrate my contacts. It's like looking through a View-Master, scenes flashing one picture at a time.

Click. Click.

My eyelids feel heavier with each click. He comes into focus a little more. He appears as more of a shadow due to the dim lighting above the bar. This place is known for its dim lighting, it's called The Cave.

How enticing.

It does come in handy for meeting random hook-ups. The lighting is so bad I don't have to waste time judging everyone's looks. I can just go in for the kill.

I can tell this guy is small from his shadow, but maybe it's because my depth perception isn't on par. Doesn't matter if he's small, tall, skinny or fat, he's a male. His smoky voice is what captures my attention first.

"I sort of work here," he says, as a smile leaks across his face.

"Sort of work here? How can you sort of work somewhere? Are you a bartender?"

"Sure. I'm used to lure a lot of people in and keep their wallets open. I pretty much do whatever I want."

"Oh really, you can do whatever you want, huh?"

I hiccup a few times. I put my hand on my chest to catch my breath.

"Excuse me," I say.

"It's alright. I usually have that effect on women," he says, sliding closer to me. "So what brings you here on a Wednesday looking so good? You don't seem like the kind of girl who would be out alone."

He has that effect on women? Who does this guy think he is? I do agree with him that I'm looking good. I'm wearing my favorite red dress that cuts low in the back with my new black pumps. I used my Hot Buns hair accessory that I bought from an infomercial. Infomercials have become my favorite late-night activity. It's this plastic thing that you wrap your hair around and the bun stays for hours. Three Hot Buns for just $8.99; can't beat it. It turned out to be a sexy bun; at least the food cart guy on Third Street told me it's sexy.

"Damn girl, that's a sexy bun."

I'm almost certain he ultimately said it so I would buy a hot dog. He snapped his tongs at me until I turned the corner. I would have bought one if I knew I'd be stood up. God, that sounds so awful in my head. It probably sounds worse if I say it out loud.

I was rejected, denied, avoided. So many ways to say it, but I guess stood up sounds the most civil. Stood up, stand up, something I can't do at this moment without falling over. I refuse to say it out loud. Just because I know I'm pathetic doesn't mean everyone else needs to know. It's not worth talking about anyway, especially since it's my fourth stand up in a month. I joined a new dating site called StandByMe.com back in December, in hopes I'd meet someone I could mess around with for a few weeks. I was chatting with four different guys and I made dates with all of them. None of them showed up, this guy being the fourth.

I resorted to online dating at the advice of my mother, who pretty much knows nothing about the Internet except how to email and how to stalk people's photos on her Facebook.

"You know, a lot of people are doing this online dating thing. Sophie's daughter Bridget met a nice young man just a few weeks ago on AnimeFansMeet.com. That could be fun, if you gave it a try."

"Mom, I'm not into anime."

"Oh, well I'm sure they have one for people like you. What's that game you like, Dungeons and Dragons?"

"Mom, I'm not into that anymore...only when I have time."

I should give her credit for trying to help, I understand that, but I doubt there's a Dungeons and Dragons site. Even if it existed, I wouldn't join it. I wouldn't want to date someone who is better than me at my favorite game, nor do I want to get close enough to any guy to let him know my private activities. I just want someone to take me home at night. I chose StandByMe.com because they have a good match rate. But I guess I'm the anomaly, not able to be matched.

This particular stand up is even more pathetic because it's February, the shortest month of all, and it's not a leap year. No bonus day to redeem myself. I've thought about creating my own leap day on the last day by leaping off a bridge.

I could turn this into a positive thing though, and make it a career. I could start telling people I do stand up for a living.

"So what do you do?" they would say to me.

"I do stand up," I would reply.

"Really? That must be a rough life."

"Yeah it can be, but it's pretty easy."

"Pretty easy? Really? I would be frightened of standing up in front of people trying to make them laugh."

"That's the best part, I rarely have to stand and people are rarely ever watching me. In fact, other people do the standing."

"I'm not sure I understand." They would look at me confused.

"It's simple. You see it's a different kind of stand up. I make a date with a man, I show up at a restaurant looking fabulous; he doesn't come, and then I sit alone for a few hours. Then of course I do the proper thing and I buy myself a drink, or five."

"Wait, you mean you go to places and wait for a date? You get stood up by men?"

"Yes, the joke is always on me."

Then I would laugh a hearty pitiful laugh and then they'll give me that face, that face that says, "What is wrong with this girl?" I'll answer them without them having to voice the question, "If I knew what was wrong with me, I would fix it."

I would fix it if I could, "it" being this problem I have with people not wanting to sit face-to-face with me for a two-hour dinner. It could be shorter than two-hours if they wanted. I don't eat that much and I almost always skip dessert. I am also open to paying for the check or splitting it halfway. Going Dutch I think they call it. I believe a woman can contribute to a night out. I'm an independent woman. Who doesn't want that? Until I figure out that conundrum, the only quick fix seems to be a liquid that severely alters my state of mind in such a way that I can forget about being stood up and just stay seated.

I take another swig of my drink to gather myself after hiccuping like a baby elephant and look in the direction of my new friend. I think for a minute, working out what it is he just asked me.

"Wait, what was the question again?"

"Why are you here alone, my dear?"

"Right. I'm here, sitting alone in this dark, dank bar, because I thought I'd dress up and treat myself to a few drinks. There's nothing I enjoy more than a night on the town. Who says women can't go out alone?" My voice rises slightly with the last question. I clear my throat and blush.

"Well, I guess that's true. I'm sure you typically fight guys off with a stick, but you just felt like enjoying an evening out alone, totally understandable. Being popular can really be difficult," he says. This guy is oozing with confidence. Maybe it's because of his height. He seems to have a Napoleon complex.

I look at him with my head cocked to the side. Cocking my head to the side makes the world look straighter. He hardly knows me. How does he know if I have guys lining up? The best way to bag a guy is to make yourself seem more desirable than you actually are.

He was probably stood up too. He's pretending he works here to get in my pants. I've already made it easier on him. I'm not wearing pants. To be honest, I have always wondered what it would be like to be with a bartender ever since I saw that movie *Cocktail* with Tom Cruise. But the work hours must be ridiculous. And this guy is no Tom Cruise. He's not a Tom Arnold though either, he looks to be more of a Tom Collins. I'd say he's about the same height as Tom Cruise. He's sort of solid with glassy brown eyes and his lips appear to be thin. He has a long neck and broad shoulders.

"Why yes," I say. I squint my eyes and pinch my lips together and let the corners of my mouth perk up into a mischievous smile. Hopefully, it looks cute now. It feels cute, but everything feels cute in this state of mind. I've been drinking for about two hours. No matter how much I drink, I can't seem to increase my tolerance. I figured I'd be good at it, considering my father drank like a fish and his father drank like a fish. The tolerance gene skips a generation I suppose. It could also be because I'm a woman, a skinny woman. I pride myself in not being able to drink as much as my friends because I'm the skinny one.

"I have many suitors."

I let my **s** continue slithering for a few extra seconds, not realizing I sound like an inebriated snake. I swivel around again on my stool thinking it looks sexy and goes along with my snake motif. It feels sexy as my dress flutters down around the stool blowing in the slight breeze I create, but I spin too fast and I'm forced to grab hold of the bar to avoid falling backward. My stomach churns a bit creating a nauseous feeling. My head tilts back slightly and my bun flops from left to right; the looser I get the more it flops. He slides closer to me as I straighten myself up.

"Good for you." He grins. I continue to squint to try and make out an outline of his face.

"I bet you have trouble picking the best suitor. It's hard to find that perfect guy. The guy who can warm you up on a cold lonely night, someone who can make your worries obsolete."

Oh God, he knows how hard it is to find a perfect guy. Maybe he prefers other men. I might be ringing up the wrong bar tab.

"How would you know how hard it is? You're probably one of those guys who leaves us hanging," I retort. I attempt to make a smug grin on my face, but it feels lopsided. The one side of my face feels numb.

"I'm a man of my word darlin'. I'm consistently there for my lady when she needs me. Most of my friends come to me for advice and the ones who are women are often complaining about men. It's a never ending conversation."

"I'm not complaining at all. I'm simply taking a break from the male gender, that's it. Is that allowed? I came out to enjoy my own company, let my hair down for a bit." And let's not forget wallow in my own self-pity.

"I suppose it's good you're alone. It's better to be your one and only guest when you throw a pity party."

"Yes and that...wait a minute. That was rude."

I try to stand up, but the heel of my left shoe catches on the stool and I stumble back down, grabbing the bar again to steady myself, my bun loosening. The world is spinning a little slower now.

"Darlin', sit down before you cause a scene. No need to get all bubbly."

I don't know if it's the drinks or the sound of his voice, but for some reason I listen to him. I sit down on my stool and throw back another drink. I can feel it slide down my throat warming my body like a torch. My face burns, my fingers tingle, my worries continue to dissipate.

"So tell me, who were you supposed to meet tonight?"

I furrow my brow. This guy doesn't believe me. "I told you, I came out to be alone."

"I can see in your eyes that you're lying. I have a way of getting the truth out of people. It's a skill I've developed working in a bar. So, who were you supposed to meet tonight?"

Just as he says that, my purse slips out of my lap and falls to the floor and a slip of paper slides out. It's the profile of the guy who stood me up. I quickly grab it up off the floor so my new friend doesn't see it.

"StandByMe.com huh?"

I blush.

"So, you were stood up?"

I put my head in my left hand and slam my right hand down on the bar. "You got me. I was stood up, fourth time this month."

"Ouch," he says, sliding closer to my right hand. "That's got to be rough and it's February, the shortest month."

"Yes, thanks so much for pointing that out." I grab my glass and drain the remainder of my drink.

"Let me pour you another drink, darlin'. This one is to being stood up."

"Okay, just one more."

My words stumble out of my mouth like Jenga blocks. I grab my glass.

"I'm sorry, but I don't believe I remember your name."

I point my index finger at him, staring long enough that my one finger becomes two.

"I never gave you my name, darlin'." His voice is entrancing. He slides closer to me, coming into the light shining over me. "It's Jack."

I pick him up and pour myself another glass, my bun completely falling out allowing my hair to flow freely across my back.

"Thanks, Jack."

13

Traffic

It's Sunday morning. I have to get back home from the shore to go to a birthday party. That's my sorry excuse for leaving my little piece of paradise. I guess I shouldn't be complaining. The party is for my best friend, Casey, who I've known since birth. We literally met right out of the womb. But I actually don't know if the title best friend still stands anymore. We're not as close as we used to be. I haven't seen her in months. Regardless, I'm going. But why a Sunday? She knows I live for these weekend getaways. Life is too stressful and the beach lets me forget about everything. I think she only wants me there so I can meet her fiancé.

Another friend heading down the aisle. Great. Can't I just meet him at the wedding? Why is everyone in such a hurry to get married anyway? We're not even close to 30 yet. She's only been dating him for six months at the most. Casey has always been different than me. When she knows what she wants she grabs it and keeps moving.

I look around me to see if I can possibly turn back. I got so lost in my thoughts I didn't realize the car isn't even moving.

Traffic jam.

I should be given a medal for going to this party. Can you get a medal for going to a party that you really don't want to go to? Doesn't that mean I'm selfless or something? There's a lot of courage involved in this.

Whatever, I'm going and that's it. Turning back would take even longer than continuing on.

I scan the road ahead, looking into various cars around me to avoid boredom and a possible mental breakdown. Call me a creeper if you must, but I'm stuck in bumper-to-bumper traffic, what else am I supposed to do to keep myself occupied?

I begin to wonder where everyone is going. I look to my right and see a frantic mother in a Volvo station wagon. Her three kids, two girls and a boy, are in the back seat, fighting. I can hear them through the window. Reminds me of my childhood in the back of our Volvo station wagon, screaming at my brothers while they stuck their boogers on me.

"Mom, Jimmy stuck his boogers on me."

"No I didn't. Mom, Liz is lying. She was eating her boogers and dropped them."

"Am not! You're such a butt face."

"I know you are BUTT what am I?"

"Stop it right now or I'm pulling over and you can find your own way home."

I don't have enough fingers or toes to count how many times my Mom used the 'find your own way home' threat. She never did it of course. I'm sure she wanted to, but she couldn't risk being the talk of the neighborhood. Nobody wants to be the mom who ACTUALLY made her kids get out of the car and walk home. On the highway no less.

I imagine why this lady is so frantic. Doesn't look like boogers are involved. I'm sure it's because she realized the kids didn't put the dog in the cage before they left the night before. I would be frantic too. The same thing happened to me about 10 years ago. The backroom in my parents' house hasn't smelled the same since. The dog has probably already destroyed her sofas and knocked down all of her expensive knick-knacks around the house. Every dog has a taste for sofas and expensive knick-knacks. It probably pooped everywhere and shredded all the pillows. I bet her husband is a businessman who has no time for his family. He's at some important meeting, so she decided to take the kids to the shore to get away for a few hours. But, you can never take a vacation from being a mother. That's what my Mom always said. That's a life long job. I don't think I ever want kids, too much drama and too much mess.

Sorry lady. Maybe get rid of both those dogs in your life.

I tear my eyes away from the frantic lady and set them on the car to my left. The driver looks to be a boy of my age, mid-twenties. He has a huge green mohawk and looks like he's wearing a leather vest. He's driving a beaten up old car, no idea what kind it is, but it's probably not made anymore. He seems to be entertaining himself with his loud punk music. His windows are open so I can hear it. I don't think I'll ever understand why some people consider a bunch of guys screaming like banshees quality music. To each his own I suppose.

He's nodding his head back and forth, getting really into it. I don't think nodding does it justice. It's more like thrashing, like a giant green buoy bobbing in the ocean. I bet he's in a band. He's probably going to the city to get to his show. He's pretty well known in his little circle. I'm sure his parents were a bit worried when he started dressing like this. He's been acting out for a while and they've come to accept this is his life because they have nothing left to do. I bet it's a bit hard to see your little boy with piercings and tattoo sleeves. His parents must be on the conservative side. However, he's a person who doesn't take anything from anyone. Not always wise in my opinion. He's really confident, probably overconfident. Get real dude, you have a mohawk and it's green.

I find it funny when really conservative people have super liberal kids. It's like watching a bad sitcom. It's probably on purpose. If my parents were super conservative, I think I would act out just to get them pissed. I wouldn't get a green mohawk, but I'd paint my nails black and wear hoodies. I bet he has a record deal looming over his head too. He's not sure if he wants to stay local or try to make it big. He's against selling out and giving in to the man, but he would like to make millions to repay his parents and help children in Africa. What a nice boy. Good luck with your band and saving the children. I hope you don't get malaria.

As I look away from punk boy, I look straight ahead through the back window of a guy in front of me. I can see his face in his rear view mirror. He looks cute and he has an orange polo shirt on. The collar isn't popped, thank God. He's driving a Mini Cooper. Those are cute cars, a little small for a guy to be driving.

He's probably my age or maybe late twenties, short hair, and he has a beard. I love beards. I've had dreams about the Brawny paper towel man.

He's on his cell phone, laughing. Wow, what a smile. I'm sure he's talking to his fiancé. He's on his way to meet her for lunch in the city. They're planning a September wedding. Fall weddings are nice I guess, if you're into that kind of thing. A guy this cute couldn't be single. I'm sure they met in college. They were friends for a few years and didn't realize how they cared for each other. One of those sappy rarely ever happens type stories. They'll be happy together. He looks like he has success in his future. She's probably a gold digger. Good for her. I hope she's happy with polo man. I wonder if I'll ever find my knight in shining polo.

I envy their happiness even thought it's pretentious. As I scowl, I look up and catch the eye of a person in my rear view mirror.

Me.

I look into my own eyes and my imagination vanishes. What's your story, Liz?

Blank.

Nothing comes to mind. A lot of complaints, but nothing promising. Here I am stuck in my car imagining where other people are going and what their lives are like and I don't even know where I'm going, other than to this damn party, which is somewhere I've never been. What is my life like? What kind of person am I? It's so easy for me to create lives for complete strangers, but I can't create one for myself.

The traffic finally begins to move. Roadwork up ahead. That's what stopped us. Seriously? What the hell? There's goddamn roadwork everywhere, literally everywhere. I pass the orange detour and roadwork 1,000 feet signs and men with shovels and cranes. I glare at them, as if it's their fault. I nod my head and give a wave. Sorry boys, bad mood.

I guess I know the bare essentials. I'm Liz. I'm twenty-six. I live alone with my cat Felix. My family tries to stay close, but I keep my distance. I haven't had a stable relationship since the fourth grade. We held hands at the roller rink. Casey married us in a small ceremony by the vending machines. He gave me a ring out of one of those 25-cent machines. It had a whistle on it. He ended up chasing another girl around the schoolyard three weeks later. I still have the ring.

I'm jealous of these complete strangers surrounding me. Who knows if the lives I created for them are real. These people are traveling with a destination in mind. I think about these people the rest of the way to Casey's birthday party while mustering up the strength to put on a fake smile.

I pull up to Casey's house and park across the street. As I get out of the car, I notice a Mini Cooper in the driveway. No way. I don't remember Casey having a Mini Cooper. I get a little excited. Maybe it's polo man. I check myself in the mirror, reapply my lipstick, and hike my skirt up just enough to show a little thigh. My mid thigh has always been pretty decent. Upper thigh is where the jello begins.

I walk in and am greeted by some familiar faces. Everyone asks where I've been. "Traffic," I say with a half smile and sarcastic tone. They all commiserate with me.

As I walk around the party and mingle, the disappointment and jealously I felt begins to settle. I keep an eye out for polo man, strutting my stuff in case he's watching. I start meeting some of Casey's friends that I've never met. They're nice people.

I go out back to the patio to greet Casey. As I head for the door, I catch a glimpse of her through the window. I stall for a minute. She looks happier than she's ever been. I haven't seen her smile like that since we were kids. Standing next to her is a tall, ruggedly handsome man. He has brown hair, brown eyes, a beard, and a smile that could make an atheist a believer. The smile and beard look familiar. After I tear my eyes away from his impeccable face, I look down just below his chiseled chin and notice that he's wearing none other than an orange polo. Crap. Really?

I quickly grab the nearest person, "Hey, is that Casey's fiancé?" I ask earnestly, pointing at the god-like creature standing next to my best friend.

"Yeah, isn't he handsome? She's pretty lucky to have bagged him."

I'm sure they notice my jaw dropping. I shake it off.

"Yeah, that's great. Does he by chance drive a mini-cooper?"

"Yes. It's his Mom's car. He has a BMW, but it's in the shop. Why?"

"Just curious. Don't worry about it."

Polo man is here, his life really is perfect, and the cherry on top, he's marrying my best friend. I turn my attention back to polo man, staring a hole through him, hoping some of their happiness will rub off. Maybe it's not even him. Ralph Lauren must have made more than one orange polo to make a profit. Lots of guys have brown hair and beards. And I'm sure a lot of brown haired men with beards wearing orange polos are driving around in mini-coopers because their Beamers are in the shop.

Casey catches my eye through the window. She starts waving at me like one of those blowup things car dealerships use to advertise. She yells for me to come meet her polo man. I take a deep breath, all the jealousy comes rushing back.

Time to put on a good face.

Pull yourself together Liz. This is stupid. This is your best friend. You can't be jealous of your best friend. She deserves to be happy.

I conjure the one fake smile I have left in me and plaster it on my face. I step outside to greet her.

"Liz! Girl, get over here! It has been way too long."

Casey grabs me and hugs me tight. I haven't had a hug like this in a while, a hug that means something.

"Hey Casey." I say trying to hide my indifferent mood. "It's great to be here. You look beautiful! I love your dress."

I spew the classic lines every girl says to another when reuniting after a long hiatus. It's polite. She does look beautiful though. She has always been the pretty one. She's pretty with hardly any wit and I'm witty with an average face.

"Oh do you like it? Bryan gave it to me."

I swing my hand back and smack her across the face. Her cup goes flying, staining her new sundress. Bryan's eyes widen and everyone at the party gasps.

I come back to reality after a quick wicked daydream. I make my smile bigger, hoping nobody can read minds.

"And speaking of, Liz, I would like you to meet my fiancé Bryan. Bryan this is my best friend Liz. My sister from another mister."

Sister from another mister. We haven't used that phrase in years.

I go to shake his hand and his eyes are like endless oceans. I begin to swim when he disrupts me.

"Hey, nice to meet you. Casey has told me a lot about you. She was really excited you could come." He extends his hand.

"Oh, I hope only the good things." I force a chuckle that sounds more like bubbling gas.

She's been telling him about me. I can only imagine the things he knows. Casey has never been one to keep secrets for very long. When I peed my pants in second grade the whole school knew before I got back from cleaning myself up in the nurse's office.

My head bobbles up and down. I hold on to his hand long enough to make it awkward. Oh, God, that's soft. He must moisturize. The sweat exuding from my pores makes the handshake extra juicy. He gives a little tug and I realize I'm still hanging on. I smirk and let my hand slide away from his, leaving some of myself behind on his palm.

"Great to meet you too. Casey has gushed about you since she met you. I feel bad that I haven't been able to meet up with you guys until now. You know how life is, it gets busy."

They both nod their heads smiling.

I just lied to my best friend and her fiancé. There have been plenty of opportunities for me to go see them. I just haven't had the energy.

"So, traffic was wicked on the way here. I came from Jersey. My parents have a house down there."

I figure I should speak so I don't look so stupid. I should at least try to make a good first impression with a guy who is going to be my best friend by association.

"Yeah I came from there too. I got here about twenty minutes before you did. I probably saw you on the road. I was in a mini-cooper," Bryan said.

Yup, it's him.

"Oh that's funny. Yeah, I probably saw you, but I didn't notice because I was too busy yelling at the other cars." More like too busy fantasizing about his real life.

We all laugh. The fake laughter makes my head hurt.

I shake his hand and hug Casey again.

"Well, congratulations. I really couldn't be happier for you both. I'm going to head inside and get some food. You guys mingle."

They smile at me then turn their attention towards each other, sneaking an Eskimo kiss. Gross.

I enter the living room where the food is set up. I grab a plastic plate, fork and napkin. I grab a sandwich and a pickle and take a seat in the corner of the room. I sit down and put the plate on my lap. Just as I pick up the sandwich a new guest walks through the door. My eyes widen and all the meat falls out of my sandwich. I blink once to make sure I'm not seeing things. Green mohawk, vest. No way this is punk boy.

I continue staring. He makes his way around saying hello to people. It is him, but he's not a boy, he's a punk man. He catches my eye. I really have got to stop staring at people.

"Hi. Do I know you?"

He has an interesting smile, a cute face. I expect it to be covered in piercings but the only holes were for his eyes and mouth.

"I'm sorry. Your mohawk is striking." That's the best I could come up with.

He laughs.

"Why thank you. It's not my usual hairstyle of choice. I'm an actor. I just came from a show."

He spoke before I could say anything.

"And you look like you're wondering why I'm still wearing my costume."

I nod.

"I own the mohawk and vest. Bryan and I were punk rockers for Halloween one year. I figured he'd get a kick out of it."

He removes the mohawk wig/cap to reveal thick dirty blonde hair. It's a little longer, bangs brushing over his forehead just above his dirty blonde eyebrows. He has some scruff on his face, not the sloppy kind, the good kind, the kind that would give you stubble burn after kissing for hours. That's the kind of burn that hurts so good.

I laugh trying to make it less obvious that I'm studying every aspect of his face. "So, you're friends with Bryan?"

"Sure am. Long time friends. He's like a brother to me. We went all through school together as kids. Now we work at the same company."

He grins.

"That's really nice," I manage to mutter. You are not what I thought you were.

"Can I take this seat?" He motions to the empty chair next to me.

YES. "Of course."

"So, how do you know the bride and groom to be?"

"I grew up with Casey. She's essentially my best friend."

"Oh, you're Liz?"

"Yeah. How did you...?"

"I study mind reading extensively."

I raise my eyebrows. Great, he's a Chris Angel mind freak weirdo.

"Ha, no I'm kidding. I know about you from Casey. She has told me a lot about you."

Guess I have been a big topic of conversation.

He shuffles his feet under his chair. His paper plate shakes slightly on his lap. His fork falls off his plate and we both reach down to grab it. Our hands brush, we smile and sit back up, leaving the fork.

"Ha, Casey. I can't imagine what she's said. We go way back, but we haven't hung out in a few months."

"Yeah, she's told me that. She's actually been trying to set me up with you; at least that's what she's made it seem like. I don't know why else someone would go on about a friend the way she goes on about you unless they wanted to set her up. You have been so busy though. I figured you weren't interested."

"Yeah, I have been busy. You know how it is today. Work, work, work."

I hoped he couldn't see the lie in my eyes. I go to work come home and sit with my cat. I have plenty of time every day to see friends, I just choose not to.

"Yeah, I'm pretty busy myself. I do stage acting and I've been in a few commercials. I don't know if you've seen the recent one for Easy-Breathe cough medicine."

"The one with the guy who wakes up crying because his throat hurts?"

"You're damn right. That's me. Those are some real tears. Only real men can cry on demand."

We both laugh and turn our faces back to our plates to take bites of our sandwiches. As I chew, my brain begins to turn. Casey talked me up to this guy and he really wanted to meet me. What's the point of the slump I've been in?

"Listen, I know I just met you, but I don't want to be dishonest with you."

"Okay," he says.

"I'm not being myself right now."

"What are you, some sort of witch and you're going to put a spell on me or something? I don't have time to be turned into a toad."

We both laugh. What a weird sense of humor. He's so strangely appealing.

"No, I mean I haven't really been busy these past couple months. I just haven't had the energy to deal with Casey and Bryan and the whole wedding thing. I'm not really ready for that step and I feel pressure seeing my best friend take the plunge."

He sits in silence.

"I really can't believe I'm telling you all this right now. I don't usually unload my crap on strangers."

"No, no don't feel weird. It's funny because I feel the same way. I felt like since Bryan got engaged he's been trying to get me to meet someone and I'm all for it, but I'm just looking to take my time and get to know someone. Knowing someone only six months can't be long enough to know you want to get married. I mean we're not even 30 yet."

"Exactly." I breathe a sigh of relief. Somebody finally gets me.

"Don't tell Bryan I said that." He smiles.

"Don't tell Casey." I smile back.

We talk for the remainder of the party about our goals and interests. It was the easiest conversation I ever had. There was no pressure, no stress. We just talked. We sat in those plastic chairs until the party was cleared out. By the end of the night, he left with my number.

I left the party only to be caught in traffic once again. This time I had a lot of my own plans to think about. Thanks punk man, you saved me.

14

Brush Burn

"Hey, sorry I missed your call."

"Hey, it's okay. Do you have a minute?"

"Yeah, sure what's up?"

"Are you with anyone?"

"Just Brad. We're watching the Eagles game. They're losing again."

"Yeah I heard. I don't want to bother you. I can call you back later if it's not a good time."

"No, it's okay. What's up?"

"Well...my Mom passed away today."

Stop.

I hadn't spoken to my best friend on the phone in about a year. We have the kind of relationship where we don't usually talk on the phone, at least that's what it had become. From the time we were in fifth grade, our home phones were pretty much glued to our ears. I remember asking my Mom if it was okay to use the phone because I knew I would tie up the line for the rest of the night. I'm pretty sure I was the reason my parents decided to get a second phone line. We spent hours on the phone after school gossiping until our mouths were dry. We would talk about the other girls in class, our current crushes, and the latest pop songs. The latest pop songs were a very important topic.

I remember getting in a heated debate over who was the cutest member of NSYNC. She said JC Chasez was cuter than Justin Timberlake. I still stand by my argument that Justin had better hair and prettier eyes.

Everything is different now.

We occasionally text for important life events, like last year when my older brother had his first baby or when we each got our first "big kid" jobs. We also Facebook message each other and email once in a while. We comment on each other's photos that we post. It's like a substitute for seeing each other in real life. It seems everybody hides behind a computer screen now and we've fallen into the trend. We were always the girls who didn't follow the trends. When the girls in our class started wearing those horrible platform flip-flops we stuck to normal flip-flops. A lot of moms got upset with those because girls were spraining their ankles.

I hadn't seen her in person since September and that was only because I ran into her at the grocery store. It's August now.

I was watching football with my boyfriend, Brad, when I missed her call. I was in the bathroom and heard my phone ringing in the kitchen. Phones always seem to ring when you walk away from them.

I walked back to the living room staring at the screen indifferently. I didn't feel up to calling her back.

"Jess called me," I said to Brad as I sat next to him on the sofa.

His eyes didn't move from the TV. "So, call her back."

I shrugged my shoulders.

"Nah, I'm watching the game with you. I can call her later."

I placed my phone on the coffee table. He shifted away from me and gave me the look he gives me when he knows I'm in the wrong.

"No, call your friend. Didn't you say a few days ago that you haven't talked in a while?"

I rolled my eyes at him, he was right. The week before I had expressed to him that I had been worried that Jess and I don't keep in touch as much as we used to. We both have full time jobs that keep us busy all week and the free time we did have was spent with our boyfriends. She had been dating her boyfriend longer than I had been dating Brad. I tried to keep in contact and I guess she did too, but I was resigned to the fact that we were going through a best friend lull.

We first went through a best friend lull during high school. We went to separate high schools, even though our childhood plan was to attend the same one. We went to rival private all-girl schools. I was involved in stage crew and drama club and she was a cheerleader. I remember telling her, "Cheerleaders are stuck up airheads. Who wants to go out in the middle of a court in a short skirt and dance? It's stupid." Her rebuttal was, "Well, stage crew is for weirdos who want to hide in the dark. You wear all black and move giant sets across a stage. Real cool." Truth of the matter was, I was jealous. Our personalities did match our chosen activities pretty well. I was shy and she was outgoing. I was small with short straight hair. She was taller with curly hair, prettier. She always looked older than me, even when we were younger. I was a late bloomer.

As for our groups of friends, we kept them separate. Rival all-girl schools didn't come in contact much, and if we did it was frowned upon. It was an unspoken rule among all the girls that we were not allowed to fraternize with the enemy. She went to St. Francis. We called them the Francis Freaks. I went to Mother of Mercy. They called us the Mercy Mothers. There were quite a few pregnancies before I started there. The current students could never live down the mistakes of the alumnae. Despite best efforts to keep everyone separate, the occasional run-ins did occur because there was one mall between both schools. Saturdays at that mall were like a wild jungle.

My sophomore year, I was walking out of a store in the mall with my friend Kaitlyn from school when I saw Jess and one of her cheer friends. Just a few years before that, I would have run right up to her. She would have been the only person I would have gone to the mall with, but this time I found myself looking the other way.

Kaitlyn stopped me.

"Sue, isn't that Jess?"

I looked over. "What? No. Keep walking."

I continued walking, but Kaitlyn turned toward Jess.

"No, it is Jess," she said.

"Kaitlyn, forget it. Keep walking." I attempted to grab her arm, but she was out of reach.

"Jess," Kaitlyn shouted.

I glanced back. Jess and her friend turned. Her eyes widened. She raised her hand to her face and whispered to her friend. She was probably whispering what I was thinking, I don't want to do this but I have to. The girl looked like her friend Rachel from cheer. I met her the year before at a party Jess had. I wore a black tank top and an orange blazer my Mom had gotten me. The blazer was a bit obnoxious, but I thought Jess would like it because it was different. I ended up being the joke of the party. Rachel teased me and said I looked like the great pumpkin from Charlie Brown. Jess laughed right along with everyone. I left that party early.

"Sue, hey." She waved and walked over to us.

"Hey," I said. We hugged. It was one of those polite 'I have to do this for show' type hugs. I'm sure it looked just as awkward as it felt. When we separated we each shrugged our shoulders to shake off the awkwardness.

"Jess, this is Kaitlyn. I think you met her at something before," I said.

"Right, yeah. This is Rachel. She's on cheer."

"Nice to meet you," Kaitlyn said. She shook Rachel's hand. Rachel then extended her hand to me. Her fake nails looked like the wicked witch's.

"Nice to meet you," Rachel said to me.

I glared at her.

"I've met you before, but nice to meet you, again." I squeezed her hand tight.

"Wait a minute." She pointed her long bony finger in my face. "You're the great pumpkin, right?"

She and Jess laughed.

"Yeah that's me, the great pumpkin." I looked down at my feet and muttered, "You get that nose job yet?"

"Excuse me?" She leaned in close to me.

"Sue!" Jess shouted. A few people walking by looked at us. One of the security guards who were having a conversation near us glanced over.

Jess stared hard at me. She had confided in me the year before that Rachel wanted to get a nose job because she was teased growing up. Boys called her Toucan Sam for years because her nose resembled a beak.

Luckily Rachel had the attention span of a gnat and looked away.

Jess and I stood there, staring at one another, speaking with our eyes. It was clear what we were both saying, we all needed to leave.

"J, look there's Pat and Mike," Rachel said pointing to the food court.

Jess looked over. "Oh, good. We're meeting some boys here. Nice to see you both."

"Yeah, real nice," I said.

They walked away giggling. Kaitlyn and I moved on to the next store. I looked back once more and Jess looked back at the same time. Our eyes met for a brief moment then we continued on our separate ways. Most encounters were like that through high school, but by senior year our differences seemed to dissipate. We both grew out of our groups and got over ourselves and we became close again. I guess because we knew the big college change was coming. I remember our graduations were the same day. Jess called to congratulate me. The conversation ended with both of us in tears. We hung out all summer before college started.

I cuddled up next to Brad. "It's probably something stupid I can talk to her about later. I'm hanging out with you," I said.

He turned to face me. "I'm not even paying attention to you, I'm watching football. Call your friend."

Sometimes it annoys me how well he listens when I talk to him.

"So?" I said in my best annoyed-girlfriend voice.

"So, she's at least trying. Call her back."

I picked up my phone, sighed heavily and stood up to walk back into the kitchen.

"Okay, okay, I'll call her."

Go.

"Wait, what?" My voice cracked, my hands began to twitch. I could hear her weeping like a child.

"My Mom, she died. Sue, my Mom died. She's gone. Oh my God, it's so weird to say that out loud. She's gone."

The phrase "she's gone" echoed in my ear. Unable to sit still, I began pacing from the kitchen to the living room, shaking my head as I struggled to hold the phone up. I could feel my ear starting to burn red from pressing the phone hard against it. I stepped into the living room and Brad sat up concerned. He looked at me and mouthed, "What's wrong?" I shook my head and held up my hand. I mouthed back, "Not good."

"How? What happened?" I said to Jess. I began squinting my eyes in an attempt to keep in the overwhelming tears.

"I don't know. She's been fine. I don't know what happened, the doctors are still trying to figure it out. My Dad called me a couple hours ago. He was out mowing the lawn this afternoon and she was in her room reading the paper just like she always does. He came in and she was asleep so he let her be. He went back up an hour later to get her for dinner and she was, she was gone. I can't even feel anything. I don't know what to do. This is so surreal."

Speechless.

My best friend had just lost her mother and I had no idea what to say to her. What do you say in these situations other than I'm sorry? I'm sorry never seems like enough. I'm sorry is something you say when you bump into someone or when you tell someone a lie. I'm sorry is something you say when you break a promise or forget to send someone a birthday card. It doesn't feel like a strong enough sentiment when someone dies. I sat at the kitchen table, my head in my hands, the phone balancing between my shoulder and my ear.

We sobbed together.

I couldn't catch my breath. Every emotion I could possibly feel was building up inside my throat inhibiting my breathing. My face felt hot, but my arms and hands were cold as ice. Brad walked in the kitchen and saw me unraveled. I looked up at him, my eyes red, nose dripping, hands shaking. I could see he was unsure of what was going on or how to help. He had seen me cry over things before, but this was different. He sat in the chair next to me and held me. I let myself fall into his arms, my right ear against his heart, and my left ear on the phone. He wrapped his arms around me. I let myself crumble and I could feel the warmth of his embrace through my whole body. He warmed the chills that reverberated through my arms to my fingertips.

Jess and I had always been different when it came to emotions. She never let anyone see her cry, not after third grade when one of the older girls, Stephanie, was teasing her in front of the whole school in the schoolyard. She had to get glasses in third grade. She was the first one of us to fail the annual eye test the nurse gave us. Stephanie called her four eyes for the remainder of the year. I remember her Mom saying, "They can say all they want, but never let them see you cry. If you don't react, they'll stop." She never let them see her cry. Jess wasn't vulnerable often like I was. I would cry at anything, being teased, failing a test, losing at a board game. I still cry at anything. Just the other day I cried because I couldn't find my car keys and I was late for work.

Not Jess.

If I ever had a problem or needed a shoulder to cry on, she was there. She's one of the strongest people I'd ever met. This was only the second time she's broken down.

Listening to her soft weeping took my mind back to 1st grade, when we first became friends, when I saw her cry for the first time.

Stop.

I met Jess the first day of first grade. My teacher had us play the name game so we knew who was who. We didn't have a chance to interact a whole lot the first few weeks because we sat in our desks in alphabetical order. At most recesses, kids played with the kids whose desks were closest to them. It was like first grade desk cliques. Her last name is Bailey and mine is Rogers, so we were at opposite ends of the room. She was the first desk and I was the last. We had a large class for the size of the school, 30 kids. There were just over 100 in the whole school.

One afternoon we were heading in from recess. I was playing freeze tag with a few of the girls and Jess was across the yard playing catch with some of the boys. Mrs. O'Connell came out and rang the bell signaling recess was over. We all dreaded that bell. Everyone stopped their games and made a universal groan as we shuffled to the doors for afternoon class. All the boys ran, pushing each other along the way and throwing dirt clods. Jess was walking alone behind them. I was walking with some girls who sat near me when I realized I had left my jump rope over by our favorite tree near the fence.

"I forgot my jump rope," I said to the girls. They continued walking, not even turning to look at me.

I ran to the tree and heard a whimper a few feet away. Nobody seemed to notice because Mrs. O'Connell and the rest of the class had already entered the building.

I looked over and it was Jess. She was sitting on the ground, her hands wrapped around her ankle, her right leg was pressed up against her chest while her left leg lay in the dirt. The schoolyard was unkempt with big roots scattered sticking up high enough to catch a foot. I myself had nearly tripped on them a few times. The boys often played war and pretended they were land mines. A few of the parents brought up the issue a lot at the PTA meetings, at least that's what I remember my parents saying. My Mom used to tell me that I should ask if I could take recess inside until the roots were ripped up. I didn't like that idea. I didn't want to be the only kid sitting inside at recess.

As I got closer, I could see Jess' tears beginning to stream down her cheeks, softly landing on the brush burn etched on her knee. It was a silent, private cry that could easily go unheard. Her long curly hair was sticking to her tears as her face scrunched and her lips formed a hard line from ear to ear.

I always admired her curls. My hair was straight and thin, couldn't even hold a bow properly. She wore elaborate bows, a different color for each day. Today was pink, the color of her cheeks. Her face was scrunched in such a way that you could hardly see her eyes.

I walked over to her.

"Are you okay?"

She had dirt all over her tan uniform skirt. Her knee socks were pushed down and little pebbles stuck to her knee. The big pink bow was drooping to one side mirroring her sad expression. She looked up, her bottom lip trembling like a fragile reed in a soft wind.

"I'm okay, but I hurt my knee," she said, so quietly it was barely audible.

She looked down at the red and purple splotch, little beads of blood bubbling to the surface. I can remember standing there staring, a little worried and not really sure what to do. I remember tearing up a little bit too. I didn't know her that well, like I said she sat across the room, but I felt as though I should help her. I looked around the schoolyard and still nobody had come out yet, so I squatted down next to her. Her body shook with each breath.

"That looks like it hurts," I said.

She nodded her head. I pulled up my sweater sleeve to reveal a Bugs Bunny Band-Aid on my elbow. I pulled the bandage back so she could see my similar boo-boo.

I stretched my arm out in front of her.

"I got this running in my yard at home. I tripped and I hit the sidewalk. It looked like your knee when it happened. But my Mom, she put some ice on it and this Looney Toons Band-Aid. It's Bugs Bunny."

A smile started forming on her lips. "I like Bugs Bunny," she said.

"Me too," I said. "He's my favorite."

I lowered my sleeve and put my left arm around her and patted her back. I grabbed a stick with my right hand and shooed away some of the ants marching around our black and white saddle shoes. We sat there together for a few minutes, both staring at the ground.

"You know what, when I get hurt my Dad has something he says that makes me laugh. You want to know what it is?"

She looked up again and nodded, sniffing up the dribble coming from her nose.

"Sure."

"When we fall down we got to get back up no matter how much it hurts, you know why?"

"Why?"

"Because if you stay on the ground, then everyone will trip on you and fall down."

She smiled. Her eyes lit up and flickered like a candle trying to revive itself. I even heard a laugh slip out between the tears. Her face scrunched even more as she smiled, her cheeks no longer red from tears but red from giggles. We sat there, both of us with tears in our eyes, giggling. I heard the door open and we looked up. It was Mrs. O'Connell.

"Girls," she shouted, "what are you doing?"

Mrs. O'Connell was typically a strict teacher, but when a student was hurt she transformed into a nurturing mother. I remember being frightened of her most of the time.

"I fell," Jess whispered.

"Oh sweetie, I'm sorry." She took Jess' hand and pulled her up from the ground. "Thank you Sue for helping her. You can go back to class and I'll take Jess to the nurse's office."

I nodded to Mrs. O'Connell's request. The three of us entered the school and I walked down the hall to my class and took my seat in the back of the room. The other kids were snickering and drawing on the blackboard. A few of them were throwing paper airplanes. Jess came back in and walked back to my desk.

"Look," she said pointing to her knee, "Bugs Bunny! Just like yours."

"Cool," I said.

I looked over her shoulder to make sure Mrs. O'Connell wasn't back yet. I reached in my desk and grabbed two cookies from the baggie I kept in there. It was my own personal cookie jar.

"Here," I said, handing her cookies. "These will make you feel even better."

She smiled and took them. "Thanks!"

Mrs. O'Connell was approaching the door.

"Here comes Mrs. O'Connell," I warned.

Everyone heard me and ran back to their desks. Jess put the cookies in her skirt pocket and walked back to the front of the room.

Go.

"Sue? Sue can you hear me?"

My thoughts were launched from the schoolyard back to my kitchen.

"Yeah, I'm here." I released a deep breath I was holding in. "Where are you right now?"

"I'm at my parents' house," she said.

"Is Louis there?"

"No, he's at work. I didn't tell him yet. I wanted to wait until his shift was over. He's been stressed lately and I feel bad springing this on him while he's working."

"Is your Dad there?"

"Yeah, he's here. He's asleep right now," she said.

"Do you want me to come over?"

My question felt cold and hard. I didn't mean for it to sound that way, but I didn't know what my place was anymore. I should have said I'll be right over, but I couldn't.

"You don't have to. I just wanted to let you know. I don't want to bother you."

"No, you're not bothering me. You could never bother me. Let me do a few things and I'll text you, okay?"

"Okay, thanks."

We were silent for a few seconds. The sound of breathing with the occasional sniff was all that could be heard. It was similar to the sound of an ocean breeze, slowly going in and out. I could almost hear the sound of her heart beating, or maybe it was just my own.

"I love you," I said.

"I love you too," she said.

I took the phone from my ear and pressed end. I had to press it twice because the tears dripping from my face created a little pool on the screen. Brad was sitting next to me. I crumbled again. He rocked me back and forth.

I sat up, rubbing my eyes.

"What happened?"

"Her Mom died," I said.

My bottom lip trembled. Brad stared at me, his eyes watery. He was as speechless as I first was.

"Her Mom. Died. Are we old enough for that to happen? We still need our parents. Who's she going to call when she needs girl talk? Who is she going to call when Louis proposes? Who is she going to consult when she needs help with what kind of diapers to buy her kids? I don't know anyone who has lost a parent, other than my parents, but my parents are older. It's more natural for this to happen when you're older, isn't it? I can't, I just don't understand. I don't want to understand."

"I'm so sorry," Brad said, holding me close to him.

"She's someone I've known since I was little, you know? She was always there for everything when we were growing up. She was there for me as often as my own parents were. It doesn't seem real."

"I've never experienced a death before," he said. "I've never even been to a funeral. I can't imagine what she's going through, or what you're going through."

"I've had grandparents and great aunts and uncles die," I said, "but they were old. Not to say it wasn't sad, but they lived such full lives. Mrs. Bailey was my Mom's age, only fifty-five. That's not the time to go. It's too young."

He nodded and handed me a few tissues. I wiped the tears from under my eyes, my black eye liner staining the white tissue with dark black streaks. I sat there in his arms for a few more minutes, my head resting on his chest listening to his heartbeat.

"I'm sorry, my nose is dripping on your sweater." I sat up wiping my nose on the tissue.

"It's okay." He hugged me again.

I pulled away and placed my hands on the table.

"I know I should go see her, but there's part of me that doesn't feel like I belong there. Is that wrong?"

Brad looked unsure. "She's your best friend and she called you. Doesn't that mean she wants you there?"

"I know, I know, but after what's happened between us, am I the person to go to her? I feel like I can't do anything for her. When my grandmother died last year, I didn't call her. I know it's different than losing a mother, but I still haven't told her that."

"It's up to you, babe. If someone calls you, doesn't that mean they're reaching out?"

I sat there, my head in my hands struggling with what I should do and what I wanted to do. It all blended together in my head and came out of my eyes in a watery mess.

"I'll go," I said. "I need to go. I'm not sure I can handle it, but I know I have to."

"Do you want me to come with you?"

"No, thank you. This is something I need to do on my own. I'll be fine. I'll call you after though to let you know how it goes, okay?"

"Okay."

We stood up. He embraced me again, holding me close a little longer than usual. My body warmed up. He rubbed his right hand up and down my back. I held on tight breathing in the comfort.

"I love you," he whispered in my ear.

He squeezed me tight and kissed me on the forehead.

"I love you too," I said looking into his eyes. I hugged him once more and walked him to the door.

I ran up to my room and grabbed my purse off my desk. On my way out of my room, I noticed a photo I kept on my windowsill. It was a photo of Jess, her Mom, and me at our confirmation in seventh grade. Jess and I smiled with mouths full of metal. I remember we would get seasonal colored rubber bands on our braces. We thought it made us look cool. I grabbed the photo out of its frame and put it in my bag. I went back downstairs, grabbed a few things from my cabinet and left.

Her childhood home was fifteen minutes away and traffic was pretty light, but I hit every red light on the way there. It's like God knew I was nervous and purposefully made me stop at every light. Cars behind me and in front of me were honking and in return I was honking. My knuckles were turning white from clutching the steering wheel. It reminded me of when I had driver's ed class. My driving instructor told me I had the grip of God on the steering wheel.

"Move," I screamed when the car in front of me didn't see the light turn green.

After what seemed like hours, but was only twenty minutes, I turned onto her street and parked at the end of the block.

I sat in my car, my chest heaving in and out.

The last time I had been to Jess' house was the summer of our junior year of college. We met up to talk about a fight we had over spring break. I had started it. I was jealous she was spending so much time with her new boyfriend Louis, who she met at the beginning of the year.

Stop

"Hey, Easter break is coming up. Want to see that new Matt Damon movie when you come home?"

"Sorry, I can't. I'm going to Florida with Louis to visit some of his family."

"Didn't you spend fall break and Christmas with him?"

"Well, sorry Sue. Life gets busy."

"Yeah, well you could make time for your friend," I said.

"Last time I was home you ditched me for that kid Bill. And you dated him like three days."

"I invited you to come out with us."

"Yeah, okay. Who the hell wants to be a third wheel? Nobody."

I had dated a few different boys during school, but Jess said they weren't real relationships.

"Hey Jess, Bill and I broke up yesterday."

"That's too bad. You'll be fine."

"That's a little harsh don't you think?"

"What? You dated him like a week."

"Actually, it was three weeks. I started to really like him."

"Three weeks? That's not enough time to be a real relationship. You guys made out and held hands. That's so seventh grade."

"He still meant something to me."

"Well, then why did you dump him?"

"I don't know. I didn't think it would go very long anyway."

"Exactly. It was a fake relationship."

Most of college was a struggle. I stayed local, while she went to a school an hour away. Just like high school, we ran with different crowds. She was in a sorority, and I got into theater. We talked on the phone at least once a week, but it gradually faded out as we both became busier. I invited her to my shows that I helped run, but she always had a sorority thing. She invited me to parties, but I always declined.

Junior year was the year we started texting more than calling. We saw each other over breaks before she met Louis, fall break, Christmas break, Easter break, but those were short visits.

She called me when we were both home from school junior year summer.

She asked if we could meet up. I declined at first and said I had something else to do, but I ultimately gave in. She could tell I was lying.

"I'm sorry things have gotten the way they have," she said to me.

"It's not all your fault I guess," I said.

"I love Louis, Sue, and I'm trying to figure out how to handle all of this. We're going to be seniors and I don't know what's next."

"Yeah, I know we're going to be seniors, but that doesn't mean anything when it comes to our friendship. And if we put boys before each other every time we fall in love, we won't have a friendship anymore."

"This is the last time I'm falling in love, Sue. I know it. This guy is it for me. I just want you to be happy for me."

"That's great. I really don't care. I'm happy for you. You want to be with him all the time and forget about me, whatever. Enjoy your life."

I walked away from her angry and hurt. She didn't try to stop me and I didn't look back.

I met Brad after graduating school. Jess lived in the city with Louis by then and I still lived in the suburbs with my Mom. When I first met Brad, Jess and I hadn't been speaking. I found no reason to contact her if my life wasn't worth talking about. I changed my relationship status on Facebook to "in a relationship." The day after I changed it, Jess messaged me.

"Hey Sue, I see that your relationship status changed. That's great! What's he like? How'd you meet? Louis and I would love to double date. Living in the city is great. We have been hitting up all the popular restaurants, so we know some good places to go. We would love to take you and Brad to dinner some time. Let me know what your schedule is like."

I scowled at her message, but wrote back to be polite.

"Hey, Brad is great. We met at a coffee shop. That would be fun. Text me later this week."

We never met up. She didn't text me, so I didn't take the time to text her. She still hasn't met Brad and I've only met Louis once or twice. She's been with him three years. I've been with Brad for one and a half.

In addition to our boyfriends, we both started working nine to five jobs. She worked for a marketing firm and I worked in a dentist's office. I often thought our distance was something that I did. I blamed myself for being jealous when she first met Louis. But I also thought it was her fault for her offensive relationship comments. To be honest those guys didn't mean much to me, but I still wanted her support. We simply didn't know each other anymore. We let life get in our way. We forgot what was most important to us.

Go.

I sat in my car a bit longer, letting my emotions course through my veins like a drug. I got out of the car and walked down the sidewalk.

244. There it was.

I looked up the steps through the storm door, the memory of us sitting on her steps eating pops flashed through my mind. Her Mom would get these pops that looked like firecrackers. The bottoms of them were blue, so when we finished eating them our mouths were blue. We would pretend it was really cold out and we were frozen, even though it was the middle of the summer. We would walk around making small movements barely moving our mouths to speak. We looked more like zombies than frozen people. Mrs. Bailey always laughed when we did that. "Look at my beautiful ice queens," she would say.

I walked up the stairs using the railing as a crutch. I could see the main door was open. I paused, looked in and saw her with her Dad. They were sitting on the sofa. Her knees were pressed against her chest, her long curly hair stuck to the tears streaming down her face. The tears dripped off her cheeks and landed on the brush burn left on her heart. Her dad had his arm around her. I could see his mouth moving, but I couldn't make out exactly what he was saying.

I immediately started crying. I held it together as best I could as I willed myself up the steps towards the door. All these years she stayed strong for me. Even though we hit a lull, it was my time to be there. She was there for me when I cried over bad grades and silly family fights that seemed so monumental at the time. Seeing her in this moment wiped away all the uncertainty I recently had about our friendship. This is what it's all about. Her Dad looked up and saw me through the door.

"Sue," he said. Jess put her head up, a look of surprise seeped onto her face. He opened the storm door. "Hey," I said. He pulled me in for a hug. The hug felt like home. I hadn't seen Mr. Bailey in a couple years. He leaned back, his hands on my shoulders.

"Sue Rogers. Look at you. You look beautiful."

I started crying. He was the first man to tell me I was beautiful when I was little. My Dad never said anything like that to me.

"I'm so sorry Mr. Bailey," I said.

He smiled and hugged me again. "Oh sweetie, thank you so much." We held each other for a few minutes. He pulled away and motioned to Jess.

"Look at my girls, together again." He shook his head and began to cry. "We're just missing the leader, right?"

"Oh, Dad," Jess stood up.

"I'm going to go upstairs for a while, Jess. Maybe try to get a nap. You girls have your time together. You need it." He hugged Jess and kissed her. He hugged me once more and made his way up the stairs. Jess never told her parents about our problems, but it was like Mr. Bailey knew everything. Like he could feel the tension surrounding us.

We watched him climb the stairs then we turned our eyes on each other. Jess looked so vulnerable it was unnerving. Her hair was in a messy bun and her makeup was leaking under her eyes. She was wearing sweatpants from high school and our eighth grade graduation t-shirt.

"Hi." She sniffed and tried to wipe the tears from her cheeks.

"Hi," I said.

I walked towards her and we hugged. We stood there holding each other. I could feel her collapsing into me. I didn't expect to feel the way I felt. I expected to feel distant and out of place, but I felt like I was home, like I had been away for so long and I was finally back where I belonged. She pulled away and sat down on the sofa, I sat next to her.

"I'm sorry if I took you away from anything. I didn't want to bother you. Louis won't be home for another two hours and I had nobody else to call."

"You're ridiculous you know that?" I put my left arm around her and held her.

"Well, I haven't been the greatest friend to you, so I wasn't sure if you'd come. You didn't answer the first time I called, so I figured you were probably mad at me," she said.

"I was peeing when you called. You know I pee every five seconds."

She laughed.

"I've been distant too," I said. "It's more my fault than yours I think. We've gotten caught up in our own lives."

"Yeah, I guess you're right. It's just hard. I don't want you to think I don't care anymore." She started crying harder.

"Don't. Don't say that. I know you care. You called me first. And you know I care because I'm here."

She hugged me.

"How's your Dad? He looks like he's trying to hold it together."

"He's still really shaken up. He was here with the police when I got here. They were asking all sorts of questions. It was overwhelming for him. He stared at them occasionally muttering a few sentences. They said they're going to have to call him later or come back to get more information. He isn't sure yet if he wants them to do an autopsy. It was a hard conversation."

"I can't imagine," I said.

Since I was young, I saw Mr. and Mrs. Bailey as the perfect couple. They had met in college, got married soon after they graduated, and had Jess a few years after that. They had this zest for each other that was noticeable. Even as a young kid I noticed how perfect they were. The way they looked at each other, the way they spoke to each other, it was so different from what I had seen at home. My parents couldn't be in the same room long enough to have a conversation let alone look at each other. They split up when I was in seventh grade, but Mr. and Mrs. Bailey gave me hope for a happy family. I spent a lot of time with them. I spent most of my afternoons on school days in their living room, watching movies and eating cookies until my parents were home from work.

"I have a few things for you," I said to Jess.

I pulled the photo out of my bag.

"I came across this when I was leaving to come here." I handed it to her.

She smiled. "This was a great day."

"Remember we went to the York Town Inn after for dinner and you were trying to spit a spitball at me across the table, but you hit the waiter by mistake?"

She laughed. "My Mom was trying so hard to be mad at us, but she laughed out loud."

"Yup, and my Mom was the one who had to apologize."

"Classic," she said.

I reached in my bag again. "Here, I have this too." I handed her a box of Looney Toons Band-Aids.

She grinned. She rolled up her sweatpants and put a Bugs Bunny one on her knee. Her face scrunched and we laughed about how funny she looked and how she looked exactly the same as when we were kids. We reminisced about the countless places her Mom took us in grade school: the roller rink, the mall, the movies, and various restaurants. We laughed about the time in sixth grade when her Mom spanked Jimmy Wright in the schoolyard because he shoved Jess. Jimmy told Mrs. Bailey he did it because he had a crush on Jess. Mrs. Bailey told him her daughter would never spend time with a boy who hurt her. We also talked about the time her Mom came in to our class in fourth grade to contest a detention Mrs. Ford gave Jess.

"Remember when Mrs. Ford accused you of forging your Mom's signature on your math test? Your Mom walked in with the detention slip in her hand and slammed it down on Mrs. Ford's desk," I said.

She laughed with me. "Yes! It was awesome, pretty embarrassing at the time, but awesome looking back. Mrs. Ford was such a nightmare."

"You remember what your Mom said?"

She nodded. "She said, 'You should be given detention for that heinous pea green pant suit you wear every day. My daughter is not a liar.'"

We laughed together, both our faces scrunching.

"She really loved you, you know that, right?"

"Yeah I know."

"You're going to be okay. It's going to be hard for a while, but you're the strongest person I know. If anybody can get through a hard time, it's you."

"Thanks, but strong? Look at me I'm a mess right now."

"Seriously? I cried the other day because my zipper got caught on my scarf.

I had a total meltdown in front of three people in an elevator. You're allowed to be a mess right now. You're being completely reasonable."

She smiled and put her hands in her lap, cracking her knuckles, her feet shuffling back and forth on the carpet. We both cracked our knuckles when we were nervous.

"I'm really glad you're here. I really am sorry for the way I've been."

"Please, don't be sorry."

"I guess it all began when I started getting serious with Louis. Life seemed to speed up. And now this happens and I wasn't even sure if I should call you…"

I cut her off before she could finish.

"I've been the same way," I said. I cracked my knuckles in my toes and adjusted myself on the sofa. "My Mom even said when I met Brad it's like I was in a witness protection program, nobody could get in touch with me."

She laughed.

I kept my arm around her and we sat there on her brown leather sofa. The cushions sagged a little from so much use. It was comforting. That sofa was where we spent so many hours watching sappy chick flicks and countless hours of teen drama shows. The sofa where we gossiped till the sun came up. If those cushions could talk, they would have hours of trash talk about everyone we ever knew. It was the sofa where I told her that my parents were divorcing. The sofa where we talked about becoming women and getting our periods for the first time. It's where we talked about our first kisses, where we talked about going to different high schools and then college and how life was going to change for us forever.

We sat there now not as adults, but as two little girls again, two little girls unsure of what to do and unsure of how to be. We were no different than those schoolgirls sitting side by side in the dirt. There was nothing else to say. Nothing else to do except be there.

We continued sitting in silence, staring at the floor, cracking our knuckles.

15

Digital Love

He said he'd text me.
But he didn't.
So I called him.
A lot.
He didn't answer.
Then he texted me.
So I ignored him.
He kept texting me.
Now we're married.

About the Author

Kathryn Sprandio Ells is, by nature, an over-sharer and an underwear-er. She was born and raised in the Chestnut Hill section of Philadelphia, PA. She is a proud alum of Mount St. Joseph Academy, Chestnut Hill College (BA in English), and Arcadia University (MFA in Creative Writing). Kathryn has always enjoyed sharing her stories with any random person who is willing to read. She lives with her husband, three children, and an exorbitant amount of stuffed animals. You can follow along with her life via her blog and view other writing credits at katesprandio.com.

Made in the USA
Middletown, DE
30 August 2023

37593153R00066